"There has to be *something* we can do, something so that the shelter can stay open," I said desperately.

Sasha was looking at me doubtfully, but Taylor was nodding. "Kim's right," she said in a firm voice. "We are going to find a way to save the shelter."

Roxbury Park Dog Club

Mission Impawsible

When the Going Gets Ruff

Roxbury Park DOg Club

MISSION IMPAWSIBLE

DAPHNE MAPLE

HARPER

An Imprint of HarperCollinsPublishers

Roxbury Park Dog Club #1: Mission Impawsible

Text by Daphne Maple, copyright © 2016 by HarperCollins Publishers

Illustrations by Annabelle Metayer, copyright © 2016 by
HarperCollins Publishers

Library of Congress Control Number: 2015958398

ISBN 978-0-06-232767-3 (pbk.)

Typography by Jenna Stempel

16 17 18 19 20 OPM 10 9 8 7 6 5 4 3 2 1

❖

First Edition

To Judy

1

"Ready to walk, Humphrey?" I asked, bending down and petting the small basset hound's silky ears. He butted his head against me and then collapsed on his side with a sigh, as though the effort had exhausted him.

Mrs. Cronin, Humphrey's owner, laughed. "That's our lazy boy," she said affectionately. Then she smiled at me, her eyes warm. "I still don't know how you manage to get him to walk every day."

"I guess we just understand each other, don't we,

Humphrey?" I bent down for one more ear rub. People asked me about this a lot and I was never sure how to explain it. It was like I just *knew* what dogs needed. I could understand their body language and the sounds they made without having to think about it. My older brother, Matt, called me the dog whisperer and maybe that was the best way to say it. I wasn't sure; all I knew for certain was that I loved dogs.

"Well, whatever magic you work, we certainly appreciate it," Mrs. Cronin said, smoothing the sleek skirt she was wearing for her day working at the Roxbury Park Bank. Her husband was a contractor who worked even longer hours than she did, so neither of them had time to coax a reluctant basset hound on his daily morning walk. "And so does Humphrey. We were making him crazy with all that leash pulling."

I nodded. Basset hounds were famously lazy but Humphrey was an extreme case. For weeks I watched the Cronins do everything they could to persuade Humphrey down the street for a walk. But Humphrey wasn't having any of it. Finally one day I went over to help. I brought a handful of dog treats and made sure to hold the leash very firmly, to let Humphrey know who was in charge. I kept up a steady conversation as we walked, rewarding Humphrey every half block, so he'd know what a good job he was doing. Soon he was prancing through the neighborhood, tail wagging and head held high. I tried to teach the Cronins how I did it but Humphrey never responded to them the way he responded to me. So a few weeks ago Mrs. Cronin had hired me to walk Humphrey and everyone was happy. Especially me. Ever since my Labradoodle, Sammy, died last year and my parents decided they were too busy for another dog, I've been longing for more puppy time. Now, thanks to Humphrey and the plans I had that afternoon, I was finally getting it.

"Today is the first day of seventh grade, isn't it?" Mrs. Cronin asked, walking me and Humphrey to the end of the driveway.

"Yes," I said, trying not to wrinkle my nose at

the thought. That was the part of the day I was not so excited about. In most towns middle school started in sixth grade but in Roxbury Park it was seventh, so I was going to be starting at a whole new school.

"Well, good luck," Mrs. Cronin said.

"Thanks." I appreciated how she totally got that you needed luck when it came to something like starting middle school. Especially for me. I worked hard at all my classes but it always seemed like I was just a little behind everyone else.

I waved as Mrs. Cronin headed back into her pretty Victorian house and then I gave Humphrey's leash a gentle tug. The dog, who was sniffing the rosebushes lining the front of the yard, began walking on his short little legs as we made our way down Spring Street.

"Guess what I'm doing this afternoon?" I said in the low tone that Humphrey responded to. Sure enough he cocked his head as though waiting to hear my plans. Some people might think it's crazy to talk to a dog but animals actually respond to our voices. Plus they are excellent listeners. "I'm going to start volunteering at the Roxbury Park Dog Shelter."

Humphrey bobbed his head, reacting to the enthusiasm in my voice.

"I guess it's the one good thing about seventh grade," I said as we turned down Montgomery Street, heading toward Roxbury Park's small downtown. It was a perfect end-of-summer day: the smell of fresh-cut grass perfumed the air and the sun was warm on my shoulders. "Everyone has to do some kind of volunteer work after school, and Sasha and I signed up for the shelter. I've loved that place ever since we adopted Sammy there ages ago."

Humphrey stopped to sniff a puddle from last night's rain. "I'm not exactly sure what we'll be doing, but I can't wait to meet the dogs," I went on, allowing Humphrey a moment and then getting us back on our way, before he got any ideas of ending our walk early. "I know I'm going to love them all, just like I love you."

We passed the town library, which was still closed,

and then the small park next to it, with benches and a playground that I loved back when I was in elementary school. Sasha and I used to spend hours perfecting our gymnastics skills on the monkey bars and keeping cool in the turtle sprinkler on hot summer days. Passing it now made me think about how excited I was to see Sasha. She and her mom had been away the whole entire month of August, up at Lake George. We had tons to catch up on.

Humphrey and I ambled past the Rox, the diner my family owned. I looked in the big front window and waved at Leslie, the morning waitress. The diner kept my parents really busy but it was fun to visit them at work. I spent most afternoons and weekends there, doing homework at the counter and munching on sweet potato fries. The other stores on Montgomery were still closed but by the afternoon they would all be open and bustling with customers. And on a warm day like today there would be a line out the door at the Ice Creamery after school for sure.

I looked at my watch and saw that it was getting close to eight. "Ready to go to Sasha's?" I asked Humphrey, who seemed to nod.

I turned back toward Spring Street. Sasha lived just down the street from me, which was awesome. A few minutes later Humphrey and I were headed up the path to the pretty blue-and-silver ranch house Sasha had shared with her mom since her parents' divorce.

I sat down on the grass next to the forsythia bush and pulled a dog treat out of my pocket for Humphrey. He lay down at my feet and began to chew on it happily. While he ate, I pulled out my phone and texted Sasha. Two minutes later she came flying out the front door with a shriek.

"I missed you!" Sasha cried, throwing her arms around me. Her hair was back in a braid and she smelled like strawberry shampoo and the lilac soap her mom bought from France. I hugged her back, hard.

Humphrey barked excitedly—he liked Sasha too. And as soon as we were done hugging she let go of me and knelt down to snuggle with Humphrey. She loved dogs every bit as much as I did and was always begging her mother for a pet.

"Better not get any fur on you," I teased. Sasha's mom kept their house and Sasha herself as pristine as possible and dog fur was a serious violation in their home.

"Tell me about it," Sasha said with a cheerful roll of her eyes. "My mom even gave me a set of shelter clothes to put on this afternoon."

"And take off before you go home?" I asked, laughing.

"You know my mom," Sasha said, grinning. "I put them in my backpack last night so I wouldn't forget them." She threw out her arms. "So I'm all ready! Let's drop this guy off and get to school." She started for the sidewalk.

"Um, I think you might be forgetting something," I said, trying not to smile.

Sasha frowned. "No, I have my school supplies, my

lunch money, and my shelter clothes all here in my—oh!"

I cracked up as she ran back inside for her backpack. Typical Sasha, packing everything she needed in her backpack and then forgetting it. Her mom often joked that Sasha would forget her own head if it weren't attached, and it was kind of true.

"Thanks," Sasha said, bouncing back down the stairs of her house.

"What are best friends for?" I asked as we walked toward the Cronins' house.

"I don't know what I'd do without you," Sasha said, reaching over to link arms. Her words were warm and reassuring, like a cup of hot cocoa. I knew things would change in seventh grade. After all, we'd both be super busy and we wouldn't have all our classes together. That was part of what made working at the shelter so great—it meant we'd still get time together, just us and the dogs. And who could ask for more than that?

Once we'd dropped off Humphrey at home, we

headed back downtown toward Roxbury Park Middle School.

"So I haven't even told you the most exciting thing," Sasha said, her voice bubbly. "I met the coolest girl in Lake George!"

I felt a tiny pang at Sasha's words but quickly reminded myself that no matter how cool this girl was, I was Sasha's best friend and always would be. Plus, Lake George was over two hours away.

"Her name is Taylor and she's from this big Southern family and has the best accent," Sasha went on.

"I love Southern accents," I said. "They sound like music."

"Totally," Sasha agreed. "And she's really funny. I never met anyone who could make me laugh like that."

I felt that pang again but I ignored it. "She sounds great," I said as enthusiastically as I could. "I wish I could meet her."

"That's the best part!" Sasha exclaimed. "Her dad is going to be working at my mom's law firm and their family just moved here, to Roxbury Park!"

I was too surprised to say anything but Sasha didn't notice. "And guess what else? She's going to volunteer at the dog shelter with us!"

And with that my stomach dropped.

2

Walking into Roxbury Park Middle School was definitely intimidating. It was so much bigger than our elementary school and even though the eighth graders were only one year older than us, they looked so grown-up. But that wasn't what was knotting up my stomach as Sasha and I put our stuff in our lockers and headed toward our homeroom. That was all about Taylor.

Friends from last year shouted greetings and we

waved. I tried to smile but it was hard. I knew I was being silly. If Sasha said Taylor was awesome, then she was, period. And there was no way Sasha would ever leave me out. So why did my stomach twist up every time I thought about meeting the new girl?

Outside of room 312 Sasha let out a shriek even louder than the one she had had for me that morning, and raced to throw her arms around a tall girl with brown skin and a hundred little braids that ended in silver beads. Taylor laughed and hugged Sasha back, the beads in her hair clinking musically. They had just seen each other yesterday so their greeting seemed kind of over-the-top, but I tried not to let that get to me. Instead I walked up to Sasha, ready to be introduced. After all, *I* was Sasha's best friend.

"Oh, you must be Kim," Taylor said in her flowing Southern accent. "You're just as pretty as Sasha said."

Taylor's voice was so friendly, it was not hard to smile at her. The knots in my belly loosened just the littlest bit.

Taylor linked arms with both of us, her skin warm against the crook of my arm. "This is going to be the best year, I know it," she said.

"I'm so excited you're here," Sasha enthused.

"She's just saying that because she fell in love with my sister Anna's strawberry shortcake this summer," Taylor said, elbowing me in a knowing way.

Sasha laughed. "That's not the *only* reason I'm glad you're here," she joked back. "But Kim, that cake is to die for."

"It's the one good thing about having Anna for a big sister," Taylor said. Her tone was light but I could hear the truth of the words.

"I know what you mean," I said. "I have a big brother. It sucks to be the baby." In fairness, my fifteen-year-old brother, Matt, was pretty cool as older brothers went. But he was bossy and messy and had the annoying habit of calling me "pip-squeak."

"Try being the youngest with three big sisters," Taylor said, shaking her head and making the music with her braids again. "You can never get anyone to listen to a word you say!"

"You're pretty good at getting people to listen to you," Sasha said with a grin.

Taylor put her hands on her hips in mock anger. "Are you calling me a loudmouth?"

Sasha giggled. "Never."

"I bet your mom is happy to have so many girls," I said, just to stay in the conversation.

A shadow of sadness passed over Taylor's face. "Actually my mom died when I was a baby, so it's just Dad and us girls," she said. "We definitely keep him on his toes."

"I'll say!" Sasha said.

Taylor laughed and gave her a shove.

I smiled stiffly, feeling awful that I'd brought up her mom. I wished Sasha had warned me not to say anything. Taylor did seem matter-of-fact about it, so maybe it wasn't too big a deal. Still, I couldn't shake the feeling that I'd put my foot in my mouth.

The warning bell rang and we filed into the class-room, sitting down in three desks next to each other. Taylor was chatting away about all the things she already loved in Roxbury Park and I finally let myself relax. So far Sasha was right: Taylor *was* nice. Maybe it really would be fine to have her at the shelter with us.

The final bell rang and for the first time I noticed our teacher, a rail-thin woman with short blond hair who was staring down the three boys still standing in the doorway. As soon as they noticed, they slunk to their seats. Sasha and I exchanged a look: if Dennis Cartwright was sitting down without being told, this was one serious teacher. Sure enough, when she sent her penetrating gaze around the classroom, everyone fell silent. I even made sure my breathing was quiet.

"I'm Mrs. Benson. Your seats are fine for today, but tomorrow you will sit in alphabetical order," the teacher announced crisply. "When you enter this class-room, you will stop talking because as soon as you walk through that door, your thoughts should be on learning

16

and nothing more. When the bell rings, each and every one of you will be ready to buckle down and get to work."

I felt myself shrinking in my chair as Mrs. Benson continued. "As you know, I will be your homeroom and English teacher, and you can expect a weekly pop quiz, a test every two weeks, and homework each and every night, weekends included." She cast a pointed look at Dennis, who sat up even straighter. "You are not sixth graders and you will not hand in work befitting a sixth grader. This is seventh grade and your work and your behavior will reflect that fact."

Sasha leaned over, probably to make a joke about how strict Mrs. Benson was, but I kept my eyes on the teacher. I knew better than to get in trouble for talking on the very first day, especially when I was going to have enough trouble with all those pop quizzes and tests. I really did try my best at school but sometimes I missed things. Last year Mr. Dunbar was nice about it, giving me extra time for complicated assignments and letting me redo mistakes in my homework. But clearly it was not going to be like that this year, at least not in science or English. And what if the other teachers were like Mrs. Benson? Seventh grade was beginning to look like a jail sentence.

"And I hope all of you have signed up for your volunteer assignments."

Finally something good! I grinned at Sasha, thinking about how great it was going to be. Sasha was whispering with Taylor and didn't notice. But the thought of all those cute dogs waiting to play gave me a cozy feeling inside that stayed with me for the rest of the day.

"Phew," Sasha said as the three of us headed downtown that afternoon.

"You're telling me," Taylor agreed. "From the way those teachers were talking I think we may have a hundred hours of homework a night!"

"And a pop quiz every day," I added with a sigh.

"We're never going to have time for anything fun." Sasha pouted.

I was about to point out what a great time we'd have at the shelter but Taylor spoke up first.

"Remember that day we went out in canoes on the lake and we capsized?" she asked Sasha.

Sasha burst out laughing. "Anna was so mad she practically exploded."

"Well, she'd gotten up at like six in the morning to do her hair," Taylor said with an eye roll.

I walked along quietly as they continued to talk about all the super-fun things that had happened in Lake George. Sasha was talking about Anna and the rest of Taylor's family like they were all best friends. Which it kind of seemed like they were. Finally I realized they weren't going to talk to me unless I butted in.

"Taylor, have you been to the shelter yet?" I asked when there was a tiny pause in their conversation.

Taylor shook her head and her beads clinked. "No, I just talked to the owner on the phone," she said.

"Alice, right? She seems really nice."

I nodded enthusiastically. "Yes, Alice," I said. "And she is super nice."

"The Feenys adopted a dog there when Kim was five," Sasha added. "So we've known Alice for a long time."

It felt really good to hear her remind Taylor how long we'd known each other.

"And you're going to love the shelter," Sasha said, squeezing Taylor's arm.

That felt less good.

"So I bet your mom double-checked that you had your shelter clothes this morning," Taylor said with a knowing look. Then she began speaking in a near perfect imitation of Sasha's mom. "I suppose you can work with the dogs but you must be sure to put your shelter clothes in a vacuum-sealed bag so that we don't get a single piece of fur in our home."

Sasha doubled over laughing. "That's just how she sounded last night," she said. "And she seriously checked

20

my backpack ten times this morning, to make sure I had the clothes packed." She grinned at me and I forced myself to laugh along with them, even though I was feeling more and more like a third wheel.

"I remember when your mom—" I started, trying to join in, but Taylor began her imitation again.

I nodded, pushing myself to stay in the conversation. Probably after Taylor and I spent more time together I'd be in on the jokes too. At least I hoped so because being left out like this was giving me a hollow feeling right in the middle of my chest.

We were downtown now and sure enough there was a long line outside of the Ice Creamery. We waved to a group of girls from Mrs. Benson's class. I couldn't help wishing that Taylor would decide to join them instead of going to the shelter, but of course she didn't. She was sticking to Sasha like glue.

But then we were opening the door to the shelter, a spacious, open building with a large backyard. The scent of clean dog fur and the sound of happy barking greeted us and I felt the tension of the day melt away, replaced with the happiness that could only come from being with dogs.

"Hello, girls," Alice called as she walked toward us. She always wore dog T-shirts and today's said "Peace, Love, and Dogs." Her hair was up in a ponytail that was coming loose, and when a cuddly little dog with shaggy white fur bounced over to us, she scooped him up in her arms. "Welcome to your first day at work. We're so glad you're here."

The dog in her arms barked as though in agreement and we all laughed.

"Meet Mr. Smashmouth," Alice said. "Since he clearly wants to meet you."

I knew my breeds and Mr. Smashmouth was definitely a Cavachon. I also noticed a blue sheen covering his eyes that probably meant he was blind. But the little dog wriggled with pleasure when I gave his fuzzy head a rub.

"You must be Taylor," Alice said with a friendly smile.

"Yes, ma'am," Taylor said in her musical Southern way. "Nice to meet you."

"I appreciate you coming to help us out," Alice said. "The more people to love these dogs, the better."

"I'll be back in two seconds," Sasha said, heading off to the bathroom to put on her shelter clothes.

I smiled at Taylor, hoping maybe we could share a joke, but she was looking at the bigger dogs across the room. Just then I felt something soft brush against my ankle. I looked down and was surprised to see a sleek gray cat.

"That's Oscar," Alice said. "He thinks he's a dog and we don't tell him otherwise."

I laughed as Oscar stepped regally around a big tan dog carrying a tennis ball and jumped up to a red flannel cat bed on the windowsill.

"He keeps an eye on everything from up there," Alice said. "Can one of you take this little guy?" She held out Mr. Smashmouth and Sasha, who was already back, happily took him. He sniffed her chin, then gave her a lick and snuggled against her shoulder.

"He's an affectionate one," Alice said. "And this here is Lily." She gestured to the tan dog, who was clearly a mix of breeds, with her long thick fur and curly tail. She moved slowly, the sign of an older dog. "She's loving too."

Lily came up to us and I automatically reached for the soggy yellow ball in her mouth. Lily released it and I tossed it gently across the open space in the center of the room. Big, comfy cages lined the walls and dog toys were scattered on the scuffed linoleum floor. Lily trotted to her ball, scooped it up in her mouth, and came running back to me, ready to play again. A moment later we were in the easy rhythm of a game of fetch. At least it was an easy rhythm until a large boxer raced over, ears flapping, and snatched Lily's ball. Then he ran back to me and jumped up, paws on my chest.

I immediately gave him the command to get down, kindly but firmly. He obeyed instantly. I didn't really mind the greeting but dogs need to learn manners and have everyone who works with them reinforce those manners.

"Girls, meet Boxer," Alice said. "Not the most original name for a boxer, but it does fit him."

I rubbed his head with my knuckles and he gazed up at me adoringly. What a sweetie.

"Looks like you already have him wrapped around your finger," Alice said admiringly.

Her words made me glow. I picked up the tennis ball and threw it across the room. Both dogs raced for it, Lily suddenly much faster on her feet now that there was some competition.

Alice laughed as Lily outmaneuvered Boxer and flew back to me with her soggy prize.

"Let me show you around," Alice said. "And we can talk a little about what you'll be doing here."

I straightened up at her words. We would be here two afternoons a week and I planned to make the most of every second!

"My office is here," Alice said, gesturing to a little

room tucked in the back, "but you'll be spending most of your time out here in the main room with the dogs." She began to walk us around the big room. "We keep toys on these shelves but as you can see, over the day most of them end up on the floor so the dogs can play with them." The shelves next to the sleeping cages just had a chewed-up toy bone and a tennis ball with several holes in it. Clearly that one had been played with a lot.

"The food is in this room," Alice said, opening a door on the wall across from the cages. Several dogs ran toward us when they realized the food room was open and we all laughed. Alice shepherded us in and closed the door behind us. "This is where we keep a list of each dog's feeding schedule," she said, showing us a clipboard. "We usually feed in the morning and at night, so you won't be helping with that so much. But just so you know in case you ever stay late." We all nodded. I hoped I could work late at least a few times. It would be really fun to help out with feeding.

"And I will ask you to give all the dogs fresh water

before you leave each day," Alice said as she led us out. "Their bowls are in their cages and we leave those open so they can go in and drink or rest in their beds during the day."

"If we aren't feeding the dogs, what will we be doing?" Taylor asked.

"Making sure the dogs get exercise," Alice said. "And love. When you're here, keep track of which dogs you're spending time with and spread it around, so they all get some run-around time and some snuggle time." Alice smiled. "Both are very important for their health and well-being."

"Sounds great," I said, and Sasha and Taylor nodded.

Alice began walking toward the back door and I noticed that the floor was really scuffed up from all the dog play that happened. "On nice days you can take some of the dogs outside," Alice said when we reached the back door, which had big windows on either side. The grass in the yard had a lot of bare patches and a few holes where dogs had been digging.

"The bathroom is behind that door," Alice said, pointing to the corner. "And I think that's about it. Go ahead and start getting comfortable with the dogs, playing and petting them. And let me know if you have any questions."

We thanked Alice as Boxer ran over to me with the tennis ball. I tossed it for him and watched as he and Lily ran after it, then raced back and dropped it at my feet. I threw it for them a few more times and each time they seemed to go after it faster. They were definitely getting their daily exercise.

After a few minutes I looked around to see what Sasha and Taylor were doing. I was surprised Sasha wasn't already in the middle of things; she loved rowdy games of fetch as much as I did. But Sasha and Taylor were up near the front of the big room. Sasha was still holding Mr. Smashmouth and Taylor was petting Oscar as they bent their heads together talking.

For a moment I got that hollow feeling in my chest

again, but then Boxer dashed over with the ball, Lily in hot pursuit. I turned my attention back to the dogs and their game, forgetting everything but the fun of being with two new dogs who I already loved.

3

"So how was school, sweetie?" my mom asked, passing me the mashed potatoes that night at dinner. Her cheeks were pink from cooking at the Rox all day and her curly hair was up in a haphazard bun. You'd think after spending so many hours in a restaurant my parents would be sick of anything food-related. But my mom said she loved cooking just for us and she often tried out new recipes on our family. The good ones she used at the Rox and the bad ones became family jokes. Tonight she was try-ing out a new rosemary fried chicken.

"Fine," I said, putting a heaping pile of potatoes on my plate. All that playing with dogs had given me an appetite.

"How are your teachers?" my dad pressed as I passed him the bowl. His glasses were perched on the edge of his nose as he carefully spooned some potatoes onto his plate.

Thinking about Mrs. Benson was definitely going to make my stomach hurt. "Okay," I said. "And I think working at the shelter is going to be great. The dogs are so sweet. There's this one boxer named Boxer and—"

Matt stopped inhaling his food long enough to laugh. "A boxer named Boxer?" he asked. His curly hair was cut short for soccer season and he was wearing the gray sweatshirt my mom kept threatening to burn it was so beat up.

I laughed too. "I know, but the name totally fits him."

"That's cool," Matt said, going back to vacuum-cleaner mode with his dinner. My mom said fifteen-year-old boys put away more food than the entire lunch-hour rush at the diner.

"And then there's Lily," I went on. "She's brown and fuzzy and she loves fetch. She and Boxer kept trying to get the ball at the same time—it was really funny."

"Sounds great," my dad said. "But tell us more about school."

I shrugged. "It was fine," I said again. I took a bite of chicken while my parents exchanged a glance and then my mom asked Matt about his first day.

It wasn't that I didn't want to tell them about school, it was just that there wasn't much to say. Plus it was a lot more fun to talk about the dogs.

"Here's something else," I said when Matt had heaped his plate high with second helpings and was digging in. "There's a cat at the shelter. His name is Oscar and he thinks he's a dog."

Matt laughed.

"A cat who thinks he's a dog," my dad said, smiling. "What a hoot."

My dad loved corny sayings like that.

My mom raised the platter of chicken. "Who wants seconds?" she asked. Then she looked at Matt. "Or thirds in your case."

"Me," I said eagerly. "It's really good, Mom. You should definitely put it on the menu."

My mom grinned. "Maybe I'll call it the Kim special."

I shook my head. "No, I think you should name a milk shake special after me. One with lots of caramel sauce and crushed Oreos."

"I'd order it," Matt said, his mouth full.

"Is there any dessert you wouldn't order?" my dad joked.

My mom loaded everyone's plates with more chicken, then turned back to me. "Does it look like you'll be getting a lot of homework?" she asked.

I took a big bite of chicken, then nodded. I didn't

really feel like talking about the whole weekly-pop-quizzes thing.

"She's going to have tons," Matt said, his eyes sparkling like they always did when he teased me. "Forget about seeing sunlight, Kim. You're going to be locked up doing homework every free minute you have."

I rolled my eyes but my mom looked concerned. "I hope the shelter doesn't get in the way of getting it all done," she said.

I swallowed fast. "It definitely won't, don't worry," I said.

"And Mom, remember, she has to work at the shelter for school," Matt said, serious this time.

"Right, I forgot about that," my mom said.

I grinned at Matt and he gave me a wink. Yes, his teasing got annoying, but he always had my back. In the end he really was pretty cool as big brothers went.

"How's Sasha?" my mom asked.

"She's good," I said. "Excited about working in the shelter too."

"I bet," my dad said.

"Hey, what did her mom say about the turtle?" Matt asked, taking his last bite of chicken.

A few days before she left for Lake George, Sasha was over for dinner and told us her latest grand plan for a pet: a turtle. Her mom had already said no to her earlier pleas for a hypoallergenic dog, a hamster, and a guinea pig. Since turtles don't have fur we all agreed there was no way her mom could say no.

But it turned out we were wrong. "No turtle," I said, scraping my plate for the last of my potatoes. "Mrs. Brown thinks they're dirty."

Matt laughed as he stood up to clear his dishes. "Of course they are," he said.

"Didn't Mrs. Brown hire a new lawyer for her firm who has a daughter about your age?" my mom asked.

Taylor: another thing I didn't really feel like talking about.

"Yeah," I said, standing up to take my plate in. "I better get started on my homework."

"Homework the first day?" my dad asked.

"We have to read the first two chapters of *Oliver Twist*," I said.

"Welcome to middle school," Matt called from the kitchen. "It's homework all the time."

I headed upstairs to do my reading extra carefully, just in case there was a pop quiz this week. No normal teacher would do that but then again, Mrs. Benson had made it clear she wasn't any normal teacher. And I wanted to be ready for anything.

"Pass your papers to the front of the room," Mrs. Benson said. I'd been right: Mrs. Benson had given us a pop quiz the first week of school. I was super glad I'd done the reading but I still wasn't sure how I'd done on the quiz. Sometimes I forgot stuff, especially when there wasn't much time to write answers. And Mrs. Benson definitely didn't give much time. "And now we will begin discussing your first major essay of the year," she added.

Sasha shot me a look from her new seat a row away. We were now sitting alphabetically. Taylor's last name was Burke, so she was right behind Sasha and was whispering something to her. But I couldn't think too much about that, not when Mrs. Benson was looking so serious. And "major essay" did not sound good.

"Your volunteer assignments are a unique and memorable opportunity to make a difference in our community," Mrs. Benson said. "But they are also a place of learning and therefore you will be expected to write about your experiences."

Dennis was slouching down in his seat, probably making spitballs or something equally gross. Mrs. Benson stopped and gave him a piercing look. He sat up quickly.

"You will explain what your organization does and the work you do there," Mrs. Benson went on, pacing a bit as she spoke. "As well as what it is that you bring to the organization, the strengths you offer, and how your presence there is making a difference."

Yikes, that sounded really hard. I glanced over at Sasha but she was already mouthing something at Taylor. I looked down at my hands, trying not to remember how Taylor had already been at Sasha's this morning when I got there after walking Humphrey. And how they spent the whole trip to school talking about fun times in Lake George. They explained some of it to me and I tried to act like I thought it was funny too. But hearing about it wasn't the same as actually being there.

"And of course you will present this information in the standard five-paragraph essay," Mrs. Benson said.

I hoped she would remind us what a five-paragraph essay was. I didn't remember from last year. But instead she was starting a lecture on Charles Dickens and why he wrote *Oliver Twist*.

I tried to take notes on what she was saying but part of me was already getting worried about the essay. I could definitely write about what we did at the shelter, but I wasn't sure what strengths I brought. And I wasn't sure I was making a difference to the organization. I mean, I knew Alice was glad to have our help, but did help count as making a difference? This was why school was so hard—the more you thought about an assignment, the more confusing it got.

I looked over at Sasha but now she was reading what looked like a note from Taylor and smiling.

I sighed and slid down in my seat. This day was not off to a very good start.

4

The walk to the shelter was even worse than the walk to school, with Taylor and Sasha talking about what had happened in gym. The class I wasn't in since I had it sixth period. It seemed like any time anything funny happened, I wasn't there and Taylor was. The gray day matched my mood. It wasn't raining but clouds lay low and heavy in the sky, making the air feel thick and hard to breathe. Or maybe it was the happy chatter between Taylor and Sasha that made everything feel weighted

40

down. Either way, I was glad when we finally got to the shelter.

The second we walked in, I could feel my spirits lift. After all, when three dogs come racing toward you, all wanting to give you kisses and play, how can you possibly stay in a bad mood?

"Hello, girls," Alice said, walking up to us with her usual friendly smile. She was wearing a T-shirt with a picture of a dog in sunglasses that said "Dog Days of Summer." "I have some other volunteers to introduce you to."

I'd been so busy snuggling Lily I hadn't even noticed that there were two other people at the shelter.

"This is Tim Sanchez and Caley Winters," Alice said. "They go to the high school and come by a few times a week to help out. They'll usually be here on the days you're working." Caley had red hair and freckles while Tim was tall with tanned skin and shaggy black hair.

"Nice to meet y'all," Taylor said, reaching out to

shake hands with them like she hung out with high schoolers every day. I mean, I did too if you counted Matt, but he was my brother. That was different. And I always felt shy when his friends came over. They seemed so cool. Kind of like Caley and Tim.

But Taylor wasn't fazed. "I'm Taylor and this is Sasha and Kim," she said, gesturing to us.

"Hi," I said, feeling my cheeks heat up as they both smiled at us.

"Kim, Alice already told us that you have a way with dogs," Tim said in a friendly voice.

"I really love them," I said awkwardly.

"Looks like they love you too," Caley said with a laugh.

I glanced down and realized both Lily and Boxer were at my feet, gazing up at me hopefully. When Lily saw me looking she nudged a tennis ball toward me.

"Let's play," Sasha said happily. She had Mr. Smash-mouth prancing at her heels.

I grabbed the tennis ball while Sasha found a tug

toy and we began our afternoon of doggy fun. I tossed the ball for Boxer and Lily, laughing as they skittered after it. Sasha was on the floor pulling the toy between her and Mr. Smashmouth. He dug his little paws in and shook his head happily.

But in between tennis ball tosses and sloppy dog kisses, I noticed something: Taylor wasn't joining us. She was still at the front of the shelter chatting with Tim and Caley. Which seemed a little strange since our job was to hang out with the dogs. But maybe she was asking them about working here or something.

When the tennis ball rolled near Sasha she picked it up and gave it a toss. While Lily and Boxer ran to return it to her, I looked around the shelter to see what other dogs might need some attention. Mr. Smashmouth had gone over to Tim, who was giving him a vigorous belly rub. But Hattie, a fluffy white sheepdog Alice had told us about yesterday, was playing with a toy by herself.

"Want the ball back?" Sasha asked, holding it up.

I shook my head. "I think I'm going to try and make

friends with Hattie," I said, nodding toward the scampering puppy who was staying far away from everyone.

Sasha looked over at her. "She's the one Alice said was super shy, right?" she asked.

"Yeah," I said. Hattie was rescued when she was just a few weeks old so Alice had thought she would be a quick adoption. People mostly wanted puppies instead of full-grown dogs when they came to the shelter for a new pet. But Hattie was so skittish and shy that the few families who had tried to adopt her had brought her back to the shelter after a few days.

I watched her now, jumping around with her ball, and my heart squeezed up. She was so sweet—I hated to think of her never finding a home. As I walked closer I noticed that the red ball she was playing with was ripped, but it made a chirping sound that Hattie seemed to like. She grabbed it and shook it whenever it squeaked. When she saw me approaching, she dropped the ball and got ready to run.

I stopped immediately. I'd never been in this kind

of situation before but I sensed that the only way to get to know Hattie was to let her come to me. I knelt down slowly and held out a hand for her to sniff.

"Hey, Hattie girl," I said in a gentle voice.

Her ears pricked up at the sound of her name and she looked at me intently.

"You're a pretty girl, aren't you?" I said, because dogs love compliments just like people do. At least *I* think they do.

Hattie ducked her head a bit, as though agreeing, but her eyes were darting around, looking for an escape route just in case.

"I'm going to sit here until you're ready," I told her gently.

Hattie looked at me and saw that I wasn't going to make any sudden moves. She took a step toward me, then waited to see what I would do.

I sat calmly, letting her be in charge.

Hattie crept toward me slowly, pausing to see my reaction, then moving forward a bit more. Finally she was close enough to sniff my hand. Feeling her wet lit-tle nose on my palm seemed like a triumph, so her next move took me totally by surprise. After giving my hand one final sniff, Hattie leaped into my lap and began covering my face with wet doggy kisses!

I laughed as I rubbed her furry back, then her tummy when she rolled over with a happy bark. As she wriggled about I felt something nudge my shoulder and there was Lily, looking at me as though asking if she could get in on the fun.

"Of course," I told her, petting her fuzzy head. She leaned in and licked me, then kind of collapsed onto my lap.

Now I was tangled up in dogs, which is pretty much the best thing ever.

"You got Hattie to trust you," Alice said from behind me. "I'm impressed."

I hadn't heard her approach but now she was right next to me. I stood up, still petting both dogs.

"She really likes you," Alice went on.

"I like her too," I said, ruffling Hattie's ears. They were like warm little clouds with big tufts of fluffy white fur.

"I'd love to find her a good home," Alice said with a sigh. "The longer she stays here, the more attached she gets to Lily. I worry that will make it harder than ever to place her with a family."

The two dogs were clearly happy playing together, which was great, unless it kept Hattie from finding a family. "Maybe while we're here we could play with Lily away from Hattie," I said, thinking out loud. "That way the two of them can get some space so Hattie can learn to be more independent."

Alice smiled at me. "That's a wonderful idea," she said.

"We can start now," I said, invigorated by her praise. I looked around for Sasha and saw her on the floor with Mr. Smashmouth, smushing her nose into his belly while he wiggled around happily. I couldn't help smiling, both at how much fun they were having and the thought of Sasha's mom's face if she could see this. Good thing Sasha was wearing her shelter clothes so her mom would never know how much dog hair she was exposed to!

I noticed Taylor was finally done talking with Tim and Caley. Now she was in the corner patting Boxer's head. Boxer was definitely enjoying it and jumped up to give Taylor a kiss on the cheek. But instead of letting him, Taylor jumped back, a look of surprise on her face. Boxer, clearly thinking they were playing a game, leaped up again. But Taylor kept moving back and looking around uneasily.

Boxer was getting worked up and I opened my mouth to tell Taylor to stop giving him mixed messages. Then I reconsidered. Yes, she wasn't being fair to Boxer: if she wanted him to stop, she needed to stand still and firmly say no. But I didn't want to just shout that across the room. We didn't really know each other yet so she might think I was being bossy. Or feel embarrassed that I'd called her out. So I turned away, promising myself that I'd mention it to her later. I didn't want Boxer to get in trouble for being wild just because Taylor was confusing him.

"Hey, Alice," Tim called from the front of the shelter. I looked over and saw a man had just walked in. He was holding a small, squirming puppy who was whining and yelping. Alice was already heading over and I followed, Sasha and Taylor right behind me.

"I found this little guy by the side of the road," the man said, trying to soothe the puppy.

"He didn't have a collar?" Alice asked, reaching for the bundle of fur.

"No, nothing," the man said. "I figured you guys could help find him a home."

Alice was holding the puppy close, stroking his head softly. He calmed in her arms but his eyes still seemed scared as he looked around at all of us. He looked like a spaniel mix, with floppy black ears and patches of black and white fur.

"Yes, we will," Alice said. "Thank you so much

for making sure he was safe."

The man nodded. "I hate to see an animal abandoned like that," he said.

I agreed with him one hundred percent. That was why the shelter was so important. It gave dogs like this a chance to find a family to love and care for them.

Once the man had left, Sasha and I looked at each other and I knew we were thinking the exact same thing. "Can we take the puppy out and give him a bath?" I asked, knowing how important it was to clean him before introducing him to the other dogs.

"Sure," Alice said. "I'll need to take him to the vet before he can play with the other dogs, but it would be good to clean him off. Let me just give him a quick exam first to make sure he's okay to handle." She set him down on her desk, running her hands over him carefully to check for any signs of injury or disease. The puppy wriggled about, eager to be done with the exam and explore. I couldn't wait to play with him!

"Fit as a fiddle," Alice announced, passing the puppy

to me. "Though it turns out he is a she."

Sasha rubbed the puppy's belly. She panted happily and Sasha and I exchanged a look of total delight.

"You can take her to the backyard," Alice said, looking affectionately at the little dog. "There's a tub and hose back there, and dog shampoo and towels are in a crate on the porch."

Sasha and I started for the back door, the puppy still in my arms. I couldn't wait to get to the fenced-in yard to play with the puppy, just me and Sasha. Finally we would have some time alone with the dogs, the way I'd imagined it was going to be, back before Taylor.

But then Sasha stopped. "Taylor, come on," she said, as though it was a given that she would come. As though we wouldn't even consider leaving her behind for once.

I bit my lip to keep from sighing as Taylor bounced up. She slung an arm over each of our shoulders, inserting herself in between us. "Let's get this puppy clean," she declared.

51

So out we went, the three of us.

The air had just a hint of cool fall weather to come but mostly it still felt like summer as we walked down the porch steps. The backyard was surrounded by a wooden fence that I noticed was chipped and even broken in a few places, though none big enough for a dog to escape. The grass was worn from lots of paws running around on it and toys were strewn about. I stepped over a deflated blue rubber ball and set the puppy in the metal washtub next to the porch. "Time to clean you up," I told her cheerfully.

Sasha grabbed the hose while Taylor got the shampoo. But as they came over, the puppy decided the tub was boring and took a gigantic leap out. We cracked up as she raced across the yard, her long ears flying.

"Come back here," Sasha called as she ran after the puppy.

The puppy looked back, her eyes dancing as if to say, "Catch me if you can!" Moments later the three of us were running after her as she darted about, giving a joyful bark now and again. We were all laughing as she managed to slip by us every time. I couldn't help thinking that just an hour earlier she was abandoned on the street and now here she was, safe, cared for, and loved. Finally Sasha lured her over with a chew toy and then scooped her up. "No more playing until you're clean," she told the squirming little dog.

But as soon as Sasha set the puppy in the tub, she scrambled to get out again. Clearly a chase was a lot more fun than a bath!

"This is going to be impossible," Taylor exclaimed.

But I knelt down next to the tub and put my hand softly on the puppy's back so she couldn't escape again. "Stay," I said in a firm voice.

The puppy stopped wiggling and looked up at me. I knew she hadn't been trained so the word "stay" wouldn't mean anything, not until I helped her learn what it meant. So I kept a hand on her and repeated the command several times. Then I slowly took my hand away.

The puppy immediately put her paws on the edge

of the tub, ready to jump.

"Stay," I told her. She looked up at me, as though trying to put it all together. And then she sat back in the tub.

"That was amazing," Taylor breathed.

Sasha grinned. "That's Kim, girl dog whisperer," she said.

I felt a swell of pride at their words but wanted to keep things focused on the puppy. "Let's get her clean," I said.

Taylor turned on the hose and Sasha ran the water gently over the puppy while I poured out some dog shampoo and worked it into a lather in the puppy's fluffy fur, taking special care with her long, silky ears. Soon the water in the tub was dirty and brown but the puppy's fur was fresh and clean.

"How's it going out here?" Alice asked, walking down the porch steps to join us.

"We're just about done," I said, giving the puppy a final rinse.

Alice raised her eyebrows. "I'm impressed she stayed still for you," she said.

"Thanks to Kim and her magical ways with dogs," Sasha said, her words making my face warm.

Alice was nodding. "I should have guessed," she said.

"It took all of us to get her clean though," I said quickly.

"Teamwork is the best," Alice said with a smile. "And you girls do work well together."

We had worked well together this time but I still wished it was just me and Sasha. With the dogs it was okay but every time it was just the three of us, I was the third wheel.

Sasha was holding a big towel and I passed her the puppy, then dried my own hands while Taylor cleaned out the tub.

"You are luscious," Sasha told the puppy as she snuggled her into the towel to dry her off.

"I think she needs a name," Alice said. "Why

don't you girls pick one out?"

Just then the puppy, still wet, twisted out of Sasha's arms and streaked across the yard. Taylor reached down and grabbed her but the wet puppy slipped from her grasp and flew to the porch steps, then looked back to see who would come for her next. Sasha managed to get one hand on her back but the puppy slithered away again.

"I think we should name her Slippy," Sasha said, laughing.

The puppy ran near my legs and I almost had her but her wet fur made it impossible to hold on. She raced away, clearly loving the game. "Definitely something slippery," I agreed, grinning. "How about Icee?"

"Or Wriggles," Taylor said as the puppy eluded her again and danced to the far side of the yard.

"Here, Slick!" Sasha called. The puppy kept running.

"That's a boy name," Taylor said. "She's not going to answer to that."

"You try," Sasha said. She stopped to catch her breath.

Taylor thought for a moment, then put her hands on her hips as the puppy circled closer to us. "Popsicle!" she called.

The puppy stopped in her tracks, then jumped up to give Taylor a kiss.

"Popsicle it is," Alice said as the three of us surrounded the puppy, who barked joyfully, clearly delighted with her new name and her new home.

5

That night Sasha came over for dinner. It was just like old times, with my mom making Sasha's favorite mac and cheese, my dad asking Sasha all about the books she read over the summer, and Matt teasing her about dog fur.

"Yup, that's definitely a piece of dog hair on your shirt," Matt joked as he passed Sasha the peas. "You're going to have to fumigate for sure."

We laughed and Sasha rolled her eyes. "You should

see my mom when she washes my shelter clothes," she said. "Last night she actually put on rubber gloves to take them out of the bag."

Matt almost choked on the water he was drinking as we all laughed.

"Well, your mom does keep a beautiful house," my mom said, not wanting to be critical of Sasha's mom. Our house was more the lived-in type, with a comfortable old sofa, piles of books all over, and the occasional dust bunny in the corner. I liked it though. At Sasha's, I was always worried about spilling juice on the spotless carpet or smudging the bright white kitchen counters.

"It's so clean you could eat off the floors," my dad added.

I grinned and rolled my eyes—that was the corny saying he always worked into the conversation when Sasha's house came up

"I'm just glad she's letting me volunteer at the shelter," Sasha said. "It's so much fun."

"Alice says you girls are doing a wonderful job," my mom said.

"You saw her today?" I asked.

My mom nodded. "She was putting up a flyer about dogs available for adoption on the bulletin board at the Rox." A lot of people in town put up notices there and since most of the town went to the Rox, they all got read. I wondered if that meant we'd have fewer dogs at the shelter. Which would be good, because of course I wanted the dogs to have homes. I loved them all so much though that I would definitely miss any who left.

"A new puppy came in today and we got to give her a bath," Sasha said.

"I bet that was an adventure," my dad said.

Sasha laughed. "She definitely wanted to play chase more than get washed," she said. "But Kim calmed her down and we got it done."

"It was fun," I said. "And we got to name her too."

"Lovely," my mom said. "What did you choose?"

"Popsicle," I said. "But really she chose it. As soon

as Taylor said it, she responded."

"Yeah, we were thinking of slippery names since she kept wriggling away from us," Sasha added. "But she didn't like any of them until Taylor thought of Popsicle."

I knew Sasha had just complimented me too but somehow hearing her praise Taylor grated on me.

"Sounds like you girls had a nice afternoon," my dad said.

"Yeah, working at the shelter is the best," I said, trying to think about that instead of Taylor. Sasha nodded in agreement.

I reached for the mac and cheese but Matt grabbed the spoon out of my hands to serve himself more. "You have to be faster than that, Pip-squeak," he said, his eyes sparkling.

"Just don't eat it all," I said, rolling my eyes. I hated that nickname.

He grinned as he passed me the spoon. "Hey, did you guys get that essay assignment yet?" he asked.

Sasha and I exchanged a look. I'd almost forgotten about that.

"What essay?" my dad asked, all interested.

"It's our first major writing assignment," Sasha said, quoting Mrs. Benson. "It's all about our volunteer jobs."

"I spent days on mine," Matt said. His words made my heart sink. Matt was a really good student. If he had to work on it for days, what did that mean for me?

It did not help to see that my mom's forehead was all scrunched up, meaning she was worried too. "You spent that long on it?" Homework always took me an extra-long time, but Matt was a whiz at school—he finished his homework super quickly, and did really well on all the assignments. School just came easily to him.

"Exactly how many pages does it have to be?" my dad asked before Sasha or I could answer my mom.

"And what is it about?" my mom asked almost breathlessly.

I stifled a sigh. Why did parents think it helped

when they got all worked up about stuff like this? It only made it worse. The last thing I needed was more pressure.

"It's just about what we bring to the volunteer work and how we've made a difference there," I said quickly. I still had some mac and cheese left but I wasn't feeling as hungry anymore.

"Don't worry, it'll be fine," Matt said, giving me a quick nod. "And I'd be happy to find my old essay and let you look at it if that would help."

I smiled gratefully at my brother. "It would, thanks," I said.

"Kim is going to have tons to write about," Sasha said loyally. "She's amazing with the dogs—everyone there is totally impressed. She's definitely the star volunteer."

My mom's face finally relaxed and I shot Sasha a grateful look.

"It does sound like an interesting assignment," my mom said. "I'm sure you'll both do a wonderful job on it." She reached for the casserole dish. "Sasha, can I get you more mac and cheese?"

"Yes please," Sasha said with a grin. "I really missed your cooking while we were away."

"Not that tuna casserole," Matt said with a knowing grin.

We all groaned at that. Last spring my mom had tried out a new recipe when Sasha was sleeping over and it had not been a success. And that was putting it mildly! My mom had meant to add a sweet chili pepper but accidently cut up a super-hot one. Our mouths were scorching after one bite and I think we had to finish a gallon of milk to cool off.

"I certainly learned my lesson about keeping my chili peppers separated," my mom said with a chuckle as she served Sasha another helping of the steaming mac and cheese. "So what else are you doing at the shelter?"

I knew she was asking because of the essay but I'd take any chance I got to talk more about the dogs and less about school. "Actually Alice and I were talking about another puppy at the shelter, Hattie," I said, pausing to take another bite. My appetite was back now.

"She's really shy," Sasha said. "And scared of everything. Alice hasn't been able to find a home for her."

"Right," I said. "And today Alice was telling me that she thinks part of the problem is that Hattie is really attached to Lily. Hattie needs some more time on her own so she can get more independent."

"That sounds like a way you girls could make a difference," my dad said.

He was thinking about the essay too but in this case I hoped he was right. I really wanted to help Hattie find a home. "I was thinking we could play with Lily more when we're at the shelter and keep her busy," I said to Sasha. "That way Hattie can learn to be on her own more."

"That's a great idea," Sasha said. "Also maybe Taylor and I can play with the other dogs while you help Hattie get more comfortable with people."

I wasn't thrilled to hear her bring up Taylor yet

again but thinking about Taylor and the dogs reminded me about how weird Taylor was with Boxer. "Speaking of Taylor," I said, "did you notice her acting a little funny at the shelter today?"

Sasha's brows wrinkled. "What do you mean?"

"Well, like she was giving Boxer really mixed signals, jumping back when they were playing instead of telling him no when he hopped up," I said. "And she spent most of the afternoon talking to Tim and Caley instead of playing with the dogs."

"She was great when we were washing Popsicle," Sasha pointed out.

My dad had stood to start clearing the table but he paused. "It sounds to me like she might be scared of the bigger dogs."

Both Sasha and I shook our heads at that. "She was really excited about working at the shelter," Sasha said. "She downloaded all these funny dog apps to her phone and stuff."

"It was no big deal," I said, pushing back my chair

so I could take my dishes in. But Taylor's tight face and her confusing behavior with Boxer still had me puzzled.

After dinner Sasha and I went up to my room.

"It all looks the same," she said happily. It was weird to think it had been more than a month since she'd been here. Usually she was over a couple of times a week. And it did look the same, with my puppy posters, the china dog collection on my bookcase, the blue rug with a stain where I'd spilled tomato soup when I had the flu in third grade, and my old cherry comforter.

"I do have something new," I told her. I was about to show her when I bumped into my desk, which was piled high with books and papers from school. A bunch of papers flew to the floor and I bent to pick them up.

"You are so lucky to have clutter," Sasha said with a sigh.

Her room was always pristine, of course. "It makes it hard to find stuff," I pointed out. "Like last night it took me ten minutes to find the vocab sheet Mrs. Benson gave us."

Sasha wrinkled her nose. "That's because she gives us so much homework it's impossible to keep track of it all."

"Yeah, but doesn't your mom have a file system set up for you?" I asked. "And your bookshelf organized in alphabetical order?" I'd been thinking I'd have to do something like that if Mrs. Benson kept giving us so much work. Which I knew she would.

"Yeah but it's actually harder to find stuff when it's all put away," Sasha said, stretching back against my pillows. "Because I always forget where I put it."

I laughed. Sasha was always putting things away in drawers or her walk-in closet, and then forgetting where they were. I could see how it would be the same with all the papers from Mrs. Benson. Really there was no good solution when that much homework was involved.

I set the pile of papers on my desk, then walked over and closed my closet door.

"Your dog collage," Sasha said, sitting up.

A lot of girls in our class made collages cut out of fashion magazines or of their favorite movie stars. But I'd made one entirely of dogs.

"I've been doing some work on it since we started at the shelter," I said. The collage had all kinds of dog pictures and stickers plus bits of information about dogs. Before she left for Lake George Sasha had helped me make a dog paw border that went around the whole closet door and I couldn't wait to show her what I'd added since.

"Oh, it's Boxer," she exclaimed as she got up to take a closer look. I'd taken pictures of all the shelter dogs with my phone and glued them in, along with snippets of information about their breeds. I used a different color highlighter on each one so it had kind of a rainbow look to it. "He's definitely high-spirited and curious," she said, reading the printout about boxers.

"It also says they need people to be firm with them," I said, thinking back to Taylor and how passive she'd been with him.

Sasha looked a little lower down and squealed. "Me and Mr. Smashmouth!"

I grinned. "Yeah, I took that one when you weren't looking." It was a picture of Sasha snuggling Mr. Smashmouth, her face buried in his fluffy white fur. His little face was totally blissful.

"The shelter is so great," Sasha said happily, standing on her tiptoes to see my photo of Hattie.

"I know," I agreed. "It makes me happy every time I look at pictures of the dogs from there."

"Now you just need a picture of Popsicle," Sasha said. "And I want to help you decide where to put it. We can take a picture of her next week."

"Definitely," I said. I was relieved to hear she still wanted to work on the collage with me. Maybe some things were changing but at least this was the same. "This is really fun, us hanging out," I added.

Sasha stiffened the tiniest bit. "Yeah, but you and Taylor are going to be great friends too," she said.

So she'd noticed that we *weren't* great friends. "I've

been trying to be nice," I said. I wanted to add that it didn't seem like Taylor was really trying but I knew that would upset Sasha.

"Don't worry," Sasha said. "I know the three of us are going to be best friends." She looped an arm around my neck. "Let's go make milk shakes."

We loved making milk shakes with all kinds of add-ins like chocolate chips or crushed sugar cookies but right now I didn't really feel like it. The way things were with Taylor it was pretty impossible to imagine us ever being real friends. And Sasha saying "best friends" made it even worse.

Still, I trailed after Sasha, hoping against hope that she was right. Because if she wasn't, I was in danger of losing my best friend.

6

Monday morning I knocked on the Cronins' door. The sky was gray and it felt like rain was coming. I hoped to get Humphrey back home before it started. I heard the sound of Humphrey's nails on the wood floor as he came to the door, followed by the click of Mrs. Cronin's high heels.

Mrs. Cronin opened the door with a smile but her phone was pressed against her ear. I nodded to let her know she could get back to her call and I'd take it from here. Humphrey was rubbing against my ankles and I bent down to pet him while she headed down the hall saying something about interest rates.

I grabbed Humphrey's leash and a few minutes later we were on our way.

"Working at the shelter has been great," I told him as we walked. As always his ears pricked up at the sound of my voice. "I think you'd like the other dogs there."

Humphrey paused to sniff the rosebushes at the end of the Vincents' drive. "Boxer might be a bit too energetic for you," I said as I gave his leash a tug and we got back on our way. "But you'd like Lily. She's calmer and she loves to play, like you."

Humphrey bobbed his head agreeably.

"I bet you'd like hanging with other dogs, wouldn't you?" I asked, turning back. The clouds hung low overhead and I knew we didn't have much time before the downpour. We'd finished the first half of our route anyway. "It's too bad we don't have time to go to the dog run at the park when I walk you in the mornings." The one time I'd taken him on a Saturday he'd been delirious with joy, playing tug-of-war with a poodle and then sniffing every corner of the fenced-in area with an old cocker spaniel. "Maybe we can go another time."

It was funny to be thinking about planning a playdate for a dog but Humphrey had really enjoyed himself. He'd actually been the most energetic I'd ever seen him.

Back at the Cronins', Humphrey took the porch steps slowly, then collapsed on his side as I rang the doorbell. Mrs. Cronin opened it a moment later and laughed when she saw her dog. "Tired, Humphrey?" she asked him.

Humphrey opened one eye and looked up at her.

"Your breakfast is ready," she said.

Clearly Humphrey knew the word breakfast because he was on his feet immediately. I grinned as I unhooked his leash and watched him pad back in the house.

Mrs. Cronin was smiling too. "He goes crazy when he sees the kibble bag," she said fondly. "So now I get

74

it out and prepare his breakfast when he's walking with you, so I don't trip over him when I'm trying to feed him."

"Good idea," I said. So much of being a good dog owner was just thinking creatively like that.

"Kim, I wanted to ask you something," Mrs. Cronin said as she paid me for the morning. "Our vet said Humphrey needs to walk more and we wondered if you might be able to come some afternoons, after school, to take him out."

"Oh, I wish I could," I said regretfully. "But the days I'm not at the shelter are homework days and I can't miss them." My parents were really serious about me having three afternoons a week to just do homework either at home or at the Rox. I'd never admit it but it was kind of a good rule, considering how long it took me to get all my homework done. Still, I complained about it a lot. And I did wish they'd let me miss forty minutes to walk poor Humphrey.

"Of course that makes sense," Mrs. Cronin said.

Her voice was understanding but I could see her brows furrow. "Do you have any friends who might be able to help? A professional walker is too expensive and I hate for Humphrey to not get the exercise he needs."

I hated that thought too. Exercise was really important for dogs, especially walks where they were stimulated by all the new smells, sounds, and things to see. Animals could get depressed if they were shut inside too much, just like people.

"I'll ask," I promised Mrs. Cronin.

"Thanks," she said.

The rain was starting as I headed down the steps and I took a minute to put up my puppy-print umbrella. Sasha had a matching one and it made me look forward to rainy days so I could use it. But today I was too busy thinking about poor Humphrey to enjoy it. I really hoped Sasha or even Taylor could help.

"I wish I could," Sasha moaned. The three of us had just met up on the cafeteria line and the smell of overcooked meat loaf and baked beans hung thick in the air. "But I have ballet during the week now."

"I thought that was Saturdays," I said, skipping the meat loaf and grabbing a turkey sandwich, my usual lunch except on pizza days. Sasha was reaching for a cheese sandwich while Taylor got salad and strawberry yogurt.

"Sasha got moved up to intermediate ballet, which is on Wednesdays instead of Saturdays," Taylor said.

The fact that Taylor had known this before me was like a smack. It might have seemed like no big deal, but the thing was, Sasha and I always knew every detail of each other's schedules. And half the time I was the one who reminded her what she was doing after school because she was always forgetting. She sometimes joked that I was her secretary. Now it looked like Taylor was stealing my job as secretary and maybe even as best friend.

"I just found out yesterday," Sasha told me as she handed over her money to pay for her food.

"When my family was over for dinner," Taylor added, brushing one of her braids out of her face.

Was she trying to make me feel worse?

"Well, congratulations," I said, working to sound enthusiastic. It was hard when my stomach was all clenched up.

We headed to our table, along the back wall near a window. In elementary school we'd had long benches but here there were round tables with rickety plastic chairs. We usually sat by ourselves even though six or seven people could squeeze in at one table. Right now I was wishing the tables just sat two, though at this point who knew if Sasha would choose to sit with me or Taylor. I kind of didn't want to find out the answer to that.

"Hey, guys," our friend Dana said. She and Naomi, Emily, and Rachel always sat at the table next to us. "Have you started your essays for Mrs. Benson yet?"

My stomach clenched up even more thinking about that.

"Ugh, no," Taylor said, setting down her food. "I have no idea what to write."

"We're working at the community center garden," Emily said. "So it's easy. We can just write about what we plant."

"And hope it grows," Rachel added.

"Lucky for us we won't know until the spring, long after the essay is handed in," Naomi said with a grin.

We laughed at that. Then we settled in at our table while the four of them began making plans for that afternoon.

"I'm sorry I can't help out with Humphrey," Sasha said, getting back to our conversation. "Taylor, can you walk him?"

Taylor shook her head. "I wish, but I just signed up for a photography class," she said. "And I'm going to need the other days to take pictures."

"Too bad," Sasha said, picking up her sandwich. "Kim, you should see Taylor's photos. She's really good."

Another thing they had shared without me. I was becoming more and more of an outsider. I pulled at the crust of my sandwich but my stomach was too knotted up to actually take a bite.

"Hey, maybe Taylor can take that picture of Popsicle for you!" Sasha said.

"I'd love to," Taylor said quickly. "What's it for?"

"This amazing dog collage Kim made on her closet door," Sasha bubbled. "Just wait till you see it."

"That'd be great," Taylor said. She didn't sound that excited about it. Or maybe it was just that I hated the thought of sharing my collage and my room with her. Almost as much as I hated sharing my best friend.

"What do you think, Kim?" Sasha asked.

I looked at some boys throwing potato chips at each other a few tables away, instead of at Sasha or Taylor. "Okay," I said. What else could I say?

"So that's set," Sasha said. She had inhaled the first half of her sandwich and was starting in on the second, while Taylor was scraping out the last of her yogurt.

Clearly their stomachs were fine. "Now we just need to get Humphrey his exercise."

I'd almost forgotten but I was glad she hadn't. I really did want to help the Cronins and Humphrey.

"The question," she went on, "is how can we do it?"

7

"So here's something I don't get," Taylor said later that afternoon when the three of us were heading to the shelter. The rain had stopped but everything around us was dripping and shiny, like it had just gotten a good cleaning.

"What?" Sasha asked cheerfully. The sidewalk was narrow as we headed down Main Street and somehow I was stuck walking a little behind them, like a kid trying to keep up. So I was anything but cheerful.

"Why is everything in your town named after your town?" Taylor asked, tossing her braids as she gestured to the Roxbury Park Drugstore.

Sasha laughed but I felt my back stiffen. "Not everything," I said defensively. "Nimsey's Crafts isn't"—I waved my hand as we passed the cozy store—"and neither is the Bundt Cake Bakery." I noticed the Roxbury Park Coffeehouse right next door but decided to ignore it.

Sasha leaned back to poke me in the ribs with a playful elbow. "Taylor has a point," she said, grinning. "An awful lot of places are named for the town."

I shrugged and looked away.

"Do you guys know what you're going to write about for our essay?" Sasha asked, clearly trying to change the subject.

"I have no idea," I said with a sigh. Every time I thought about it my mind became a gigantic blank.

"But you do so much with the dogs," Sasha said.

"I know, but I'm not really sure how to make that

into an essay," I said. "I just like playing with dogs."

"I was thinking we could write about Popsicle," Taylor said, sidestepping a puddle on the sidewalk. "Like how we helped out with washing her and named her and stuff."

"Oh, good idea," Sasha said. Her hair was loose today and it blew in the slight wind.

"We can't all write the same thing," I pointed out. We were passing the Ice Creamery, another store not named after Roxbury Park. I couldn't help thinking about the start of the summer, when it had been just me and Sasha getting ice cream and then going to the park.

"Right," Taylor said. Her shoulders slumped a little.

"Here we are," Sasha said brightly, opening the door of the shelter.

As soon as she saw us, Lily ran over, panting happily, and my mood lifted instantly. I knelt down and gave her a good rub.

"Hello, girls," Alice said. Her ponytail seemed to

have more hair falling out of it than usual. "How was school today?"

Sasha answered and as I listened I realized there was an unusual sound in the shelter. Along with the normal barking, scuffles from play, and Tim and Caley chatting in the corner, there was a whining sound. Something was wrong with one of the dogs.

"Are all the dogs okay, Alice?" I asked. As I spoke I realized I had interrupted Taylor but I was too worried about the upset dog to apologize.

Alice sighed. "Popsicle has been having a hard time," she admitted. "And honestly I have too. She won't stop crying, she's scared of everything, and she wants attention all the time."

Sure enough I realized that the sound came from Tim and Caley's corner, where they weren't chatting; they were both comforting the small black and white puppy.

"A puppy is a lot of work," Alice said. "I'm worried it was a mistake to take her in. Puppies adopt out much faster than older dogs, and I really need to be focused on finding homes for the others."

"But where would she go?" Sasha asked in a small voice.

I realized I was holding my breath as we waited for Alice's answer.

Alice smiled. "Don't worry, we'll keep her," she said. She looked over to where Tim was now cradling Popsicle in his arms. "She's too sweet to resist. We'll just have to double our efforts to find homes for the older dogs."

I saw Sasha's brows draw together and I wondered if she was confused about the same thing I was. "Is there a rush to adopt out the dogs?" she asked.

Yeah, exactly what I had been thinking.

Alice's face seemed to fall just a bit but maybe I was imagining it because her voice was cheerful. "I just want them to find homes," she said. "Don't worry."

But as I watched her take out a leash and head over to Popsicle, I couldn't help but feel like things weren't quite right. Between Humphrey and Popsicle it seemed like there was a lot to worry about.

"Hey, guys," Caley said as she and Tim came up to us, Boxer and Hattie following close behind. Tim tossed a ratty tennis ball and both dogs flew after it.

It suddenly occurred to me that maybe one of them could walk Humphrey after school. I cleared my throat, wondering how to best ask. They were always super friendly, but I still felt kind of intimidated talking to high schoolers like they were just regular kids. "Um, one of my neighbors needs someone to walk their dog after school," I said, feeling my cheeks heat up as I spoke. I probably looked like a little kid but I pushed ahead. "None of us could do it but would either of you guys maybe be interested?" And now I definitely sounded like a little kid.

But Tim and Caley were both just shaking their heads reluctantly.

"I wish I could but I'm in drama club the afternoons I'm not here," Caley said.

Tim grinned. "She always gets the lead in the school play."

"Not always," Caley said, but the way her eyes sparkled told me Tim was probably right.

"I'd love to do it," Tim said, running a hand through his black hair. "But I take computer programming classes twice a week."

"I hope you can find someone to help," Caley said, looking concerned.

I nodded. "Thanks," I said.

Boxer and Lily raced up with the ball, almost crashing into us.

"There's a lot of energy here," Caley said, laughing. "Let's take these guys outside to run around."

Running around with dogs sounded fantastic to me. I headed for the back door and the second I opened it Lily was out like a shot, with Hattie on her heels. I followed, laughing. There was a cool breeze that felt good on my warm cheeks.

"Let's try to separate Lily and Hattie," I said.

"Right," Sasha said. She picked up a tennis ball and threw it for Lily while I distracted Hattie with a green Frisbee. I threw it for her in the opposite direction and after a moment she took off after it. A second later, Boxer, who had come out right behind me, beat her to it. He snatched up the prize in his mouth and began prancing in circles, Hattie running happily behind him.

I took off after them, Mr. Smashmouth at my heels. It was amazing how much he could do despite being unable to see. He was clearly using his other senses to know where we were and what the action was around him.

I grabbed the Frisbee and began to play tug-of-war with Boxer and Hattie. A moment later Sasha came up, still playing fetch with Lily. I managed to get the Frisbee free and sent it flying across the yard, Hattie and Boxer racing after it. They came racing back, followed by Lily, who set her ball at Sasha's feet and then jumped on her joyfully. Hattie and Boxer immediately jumped up on me, Mr. Smashmouth right behind them. Sasha and I were cracking up as we tried to cuddle all four dogs at once. It was perfect. Exactly how I imagined it would be, back before Taylor. And that made me realize that it was strange she wasn't here, in the middle of the action, with us.

I glanced around the yard and saw that she was still on the porch, playing with her phone. The way she was standing was stiff, as though she felt awkward, and her braids, which she usually kept back neatly, were falling over her face. It was very different from the Taylor at school and the one who chatted so easily with Caley and Tim.

Was she feeling left out? I knew how bad that felt. And I didn't want anyone, even Taylor, to have that feeling. So I untangled myself from the dogs, brushed a stray leaf out of my hair, and walked over to her.

"Taylor, come play with us," I said.

Taylor looked down at her feet. "Um, thanks but I need to watch the door, to make sure the dogs all stay outside."

For a moment I felt annoyed, like she just didn't want to help out. But then I watched Taylor for a moment, the way the corners of her mouth turned down and her eyes kept darting at the dogs. And I realized my dad was right.

"You're scared of the dogs," I blurted out.

Taylor's face instantly hardened. "I am not," she said.

I took a deep breath. This wasn't going well and I really needed to understand what was going on with Taylor. Otherwise it would never feel right to have her here.

"Sometimes it looks like you're not totally comfortable here," I said gently.

But Taylor's face remained hard. "I'm fine," she snapped. "Not everyone talks to dogs like they're people."

"True, but it seems like you never want to play with the dogs," I said, making sure my voice did not sound accusing. I honestly just wanted to know what was going on.

"I play with them," she said defensively.

"It looks like they make you anxious," I said. I was ready to give up. If she didn't want to talk to me I couldn't force her.

But then Taylor's shoulders slumped and she sighed. "You're right," she said, her eyes downcast. "I'm okay with little dogs, and puppies like Popsicle. But big dogs like Lily and Boxer make me nervous."

I reached out and touched her arm, glad she had trusted me with the truth.

She gave me a sad smile. "I was worried about it when Sasha asked me to volunteer here with you guys," she said. "But I really like Sasha and I wanted to be with her. Plus, the way she talked about you, like we'd all be such great friends, it sounded too fun to pass up."

I felt a prick of guilt at her words. True, I'd felt left out a lot, but maybe I hadn't tried that hard. After all, Taylor was the one who'd had to leave her home and all her friends to live here. I probably could have helped Taylor more instead of just pulling away. And trying to pull Sasha with me.

"I *do* like the shelter," Taylor was saying. "I just don't like it when Boxer jumps on me. And I'm not like you—I don't know what to do when Hattie gets nervous."

Maybe I hadn't helped enough before but I could help now. "I totally understand," I said, linking my arm through hers. "But all you need is to show the dogs who's in charge. It all falls into place after that. I'll show you."

"Really?" she asked, arching an eyebrow.

I grinned. "I'm the dog whisperer, remember? Trust me!"

Taylor laughed.

"Okay, so the first thing is how you feel," I said. "You need to believe that you are the boss. Because if you don't believe it, the dogs won't either. And even if you don't believe it, fake it like you do."

"I can do that," Taylor said. "The faking it anyway."

"Next is giving commands like you mean them," I

said. "Dogs recognize certain words, like 'no' or 'sit.'" I remembered Humphrey. "Or 'breakfast,'" I added with a grin. "But it's not just the words they respond to. It's your tone of voice."

Taylor was nodding. "That makes sense," she said.

"It's all in your attitude, really," I said. "Let them know you're in charge and they'll listen, without getting wild."

"That would be great," Taylor said. I suddenly realized how hard these past days at the shelter must have been for her. Plus her anxiety had probably made the dogs act up even more around her, making it all even worse. But what was cool was that we were about to change all that.

"Okay, let's give it a try," I said, steering us over to a quiet corner of the yard. "We'll start with Lily."

Taylor bit her lip, then nodded. I called Lily over to us. She bounded up to me and jumped up to give me a kiss. "Sit," I said firmly. Lily sat. I turned to Taylor. "Your turn."

Taylor took a few steps away, then took a deep breath. "Lily, come," she said, her voice a little shaky.

Lily cocked her head but didn't move.

"See?" Taylor said to me. "I don't know how to do it."

I thought for a second. "Pretend Lily is your older sister Anna and you're telling her to stop bossing you around."

Taylor's eyes lit up. "Lily, come," she commanded in a strong, firm voice.

Lily went right to Taylor, wagging her tail and looking up at her.

"Tell her she's a good dog," I said. "Dogs need to know when they do a good job."

"Just like us," Taylor mused as she reached down and stroked Lily's fuzzy brown head. "Good dog, Lily."

The praise pleased Lily so much she gave a short bark and jumped up to play with Taylor. Taylor immediately took a step back, just like she had done before with Boxer.

"You're giving her a mixed message," I said as Lily jumped again. "She thinks you're playing. So if you're not, tell her."

"No," Taylor said as Lily jumped again. "No."

Lily stopped.

"Sit," Taylor said.

And Lily sat.

"You're getting the hang of it," I said, thrilled it was working.

Taylor beamed. "That Anna voice really does the trick, doesn't it?" she said proudly.

We walked back toward the center of the yard, where Sasha was throwing the Frisbee for Boxer and Hattie. Mr. Smashmouth sat at her feet, panting happily.

"I'm sorry if I've been pushing you away," I said quietly. "And trying to keep Sasha for myself. It's just that it's always been the two of us, you know?"

Taylor nodded seriously, then cracked a smile. "Looks like someone needs to work on improving her sharing skills," she said in a perfect imitation of Mrs. Benson.

I laughed and any last tension between me and Taylor flew away in the breeze blowing through the yard.

"And I should apologize for not telling you guys I was scared of big dogs," she said. "Especially since you could have taught me your dog whispering magic last week and then I wouldn't have worried all weekend about being eaten by Boxer!"

I laughed again. "He's just a big, harmless sweetie, I promise," I said. "Are you ready to hang out with him now?" We were nearing Sasha and the dogs.

Taylor rested a hand on Lily, who was not leaving her side. "Let's do it," she said.

So we headed into the fray. I took the Frisbee from Sasha, who gave me a questioning look. I nodded and smiled to show that everything was good with me and Taylor, then threw the Frisbee for Boxer and Hattie. They raced after it while Mr. Smashmouth got to his feet to greet Taylor. She bent down and rubbed his fluffy head. Hattie and Boxer came flying back and I saw Taylor stiffen. But then Lily nudged her and Taylor buried her hands in Lily's thick fur. I could tell it calmed her to be with Lily by the way her whole body relaxed. I reached over and gave Lily's ear an affectionate scratch. Sure, I'd given some pointers, but the real teachers were the dogs themselves. It might take some time but I knew Taylor and Boxer would be fine. Just like me and Taylor were finally going to be fine.

Caley came over with a ball that she threw for Hattie. Seeing her reminded me of earlier with Popsicle and the things that Alice had said.

"Did you guys think Alice looked really stressed before?" I asked as I snuggled with Mr. Smashmouth.

Taylor, who was still petting Lily, nodded. "Something doesn't feel right at the shelter," she said. "So much of the stuff here is old and run-down."

Boxer was back with his Frisbee and Taylor was right, it was old. It was covered with bite marks and a piece of the rim was torn off. A lot of the toys were the same, plus there were those holes in the fence. But I hated to hear anything critical about the shelter. "Alice probably doesn't have a lot of funding to get new things all the time," I said.

"You're right," Caley said. Her face was somber. "But it's actually worse than not having enough money for new toys."

An icy shiver traveled down my spine. "What do you mean, worse?" I asked, almost not wanting to know the answer.

"You guys know the shelter runs on donations," Caley said. "But for a while now there haven't been enough of them to cover even the basics, like rent and dog food. Alice has been doing fund-raising but so far she hasn't been able to bring in much at all."

"So what does that mean?" Sasha asked, her eyes wide.

"What it means is that Alice might be forced to close the shelter," Caley said. "That's why she's trying so hard to find homes for the dogs."

"What happens if she doesn't?" Taylor asked, her

hands resting protectively on Lily.

"They'd have to go to the no-kill shelter in Preston," Caley said.

I couldn't believe what I was hearing. "The shelter can't close!" I cried.

I could see tears in Sasha's eyes at the thought and my own eyes were hot and prickly.

"It's really sad," Caley said. "But if Alice can't raise the money, there's nothing else to be done."

"There has to be *something* we can do, something so that the shelter can stay open," I said desperately.

Sasha was looking at me doubtfully and I knew what she was thinking: If Alice couldn't find a way to keep the shelter open, how could we?

But Taylor was nodding. "Kim's right," she said in her firm Anna voice. "We are going to find a way to save the shelter."

8

A black cloud hung over our last hour at the shelter. Every time I threw the Frisbee for Boxer and Hattie and watched them run, my heart ached. What would happen to them at a big city shelter? And then there was Mr. Smashmouth, who was blind. Who would look out for him? I knew the workers at the city shelter would be kind, but it was crowded and understaffed. The dogs would never get the love and care they got here. It was just so unfair.

The three of us were subdued as we said good-bye to Alice, who was in the middle of sending out an email blast about the dogs ready for adoption. Then we headed out. The sun was bright but the air had a nip of fall that had me a little shivery. Or maybe it was just the thought of the shelter having to close that had me hugging myself as we stood out on the sidewalk.

"I'll see you guys tomorrow," Sasha said, her normally bouncy voice flat.

"Bye," I said. I was heading home to squeeze in some homework before dinner.

"See you, Kim," Taylor said. Then she smiled at me. "And thanks for the dog tips."

At that Sasha's eyes lit up a bit and she gave me a thumbs-up. I could tell she was happy Taylor and I were finally friends.

I smiled back at both of them though my heart wasn't totally in it. Of course I was really glad Taylor and I were going to be friends now, but even that was overshadowed by the news about the shelter.

Still, as I started walking home I reminded myself that our new friendship was one good thing that had happened today. That was something my mom taught me, to remember the good things that happened, not just worry about the one thing going wrong. She called it big-picture thinking but what I liked was that it always made my problem feel a little smaller and more manageable. Though it was unlikely that would happen with this problem.

"Hi, Kim," my mom called from the kitchen when I walked in the front door a few minutes later.

"How did you know it was me and not Matt?" I asked, dropping my backpack at the foot of the stairs and heading in for a snack.

My mom smiled at me when I walked in. "Matt sounds like a herd of cattle when he comes in," she said. "You're a little quieter."

"Like maybe just one or two cows?" I asked.

My mom laughed. "Exactly."

I grabbed an apple from the fruit bowl and sat

on one of the stools at the island in the center of our kitchen. Our kitchen was big, with a fancy stove and fridge, which you'd pretty much expect from people who worked with food all day. But the counter was worn and the sage green walls were faded so it matched the lived-in feel of the rest of the house. The fridge was still covered with pictures Matt and I had drawn in grade school, some fraying and yellowed around the edges. They were held up with alphabet magnets, the kind little kids use to learn the letters. We kept telling my mom to get rid of all of it, since we're a lot older now and draw better pictures. And know the alphabet. But my mom insisted she loved the reminders of when we were little.

"Don't ruin your appetite," my mom said as I crunched into my apple. "I'm making lasagna."

Lasagna was one of my favorites. "Sounds good," I said. "I'll stop after this."

My mom's eyes narrowed. "What's bothering you, sweetie?" she asked.

Sometimes it annoyed me that my mom could so totally read my mind, but right now it was kind of a relief.

"Well, first of all, I feel bad because the Cronins need someone to walk Humphrey in the afternoons and I can't help," I said.

My mom was washing lettuce for a salad but she paused to raise an eyebrow at me. "Is this your way of asking if you can take a homework afternoon to walk him? Because I think you know the answer to that."

"No, I'm not asking," I said. "I just feel sad for poor Humphrey being home alone all day."

My mom frowned. "It is too bad," she said sympathetically. My parents wouldn't let me have a dog because they were so busy but they did really like animals and I knew she felt sad for Humphrey too.

"Even worse than that is the problem at the shelter," I went on, tossing my apple core in the garbage. "It might have to close."

"Oh, no," my mom exclaimed. "Why?"

I explained what Caley had told us.

"That's awful," my mom said, shaking her head. "I really hope Alice can figure something out."

"Me too," I said. I was kind of hoping my mom would come up with a great idea but she just went back to chopping up cucumbers for the salad.

"I wonder if we could have a bake sale," I said. "Or some other kind of fund-raiser."

My mom turned to me with a sad smile. "I know you want to help," she said. "But if the shelter is in jeopardy of closing, it's going to take more than a few hundred dollars to save it."

I slumped a little on the stool.

"I think Alice needs real money coming in," my mom said. "A grant or another steady source of income. And I don't think that's something you girls can come up with, much as I know you'd like to."

I sighed. My mom was probably right. Taylor was nice to believe in us but really this problem was too big for me and my friends to solve.

"Alice is awfully good at her job," my mom said as I got up, ready to get some homework done before dinner. "I wouldn't be surprised if she found a way out of this mess."

"I bet you're right," I said.

But as I grabbed my backpack from the floor where I'd left it and headed upstairs, I wasn't so sure. Caley had seemed convinced things were dire and Alice had looked so tense.

I hated to even think it, but it looked like there was a very good chance the Roxbury Park Dog Shelter was going to have to close its doors for good.

The three of us were gloomy as we sat in the cafeteria the next day, and it wasn't because of the yucky smell of boiled brussels sprouts. Though obviously that didn't help.

"So do you guys have any ideas about how we can save the shelter?" Sasha asked. Today her cheese sandwich was untouched.

"Last year at my old school we had a car wash to raise money for the spring festival," Taylor said. She was stirring her yogurt but hadn't taken a bite.

Sasha perked up. "Maybe we could do that here," she said. "I mean, everyone has cars and they have to wash them sometime. Why not for a good cause?"

I shook my head, remembering what my mom had said last night. "I don't think a few hundred dollars is enough," I said. "Like if Alice can't make the rent she needs money coming in regularly, not just once after a bake sale or car wash."

Taylor sighed. "That makes sense," she said. "But I can't even figure out how to earn money for a new camera. I have no idea how to save a whole dog shelter."

"Maybe we could do one fund-raiser a month?" Sasha asked. "Like a car wash this month, then a bake sale, and something else after that."

"We might run out of 'somethings' though," Taylor said.

"And people might get tired of giving us money

every month," I added.

"Yeah, you're probably right," Sasha said. "I guess we'll just have to keep thinking."

"Hey, do you guys want some cookies?" Rachel asked, leaning over from the table next to us and holding up a big plastic Tupperware. "We baked them yesterday and we have way too many."

Taylor grinned, though the corners of her mouth didn't go up as high as usual. "I think we can help you with that problem," she said.

The four of them pulled their chairs over and soon we were all eating oatmeal chocolate chip cookies and complaining about the test Mrs. Benson was giving us in science the next day.

But even as I picked at a cookie and chimed in once in a while, I couldn't stop thinking about the shelter and how awful it would be if it was gone.

That afternoon Taylor had photography class and Sasha was headed off to dance, so I walked into town by myself for my homework afternoon at the Rox. Mrs. Benson had handed back our latest pop quizzes and I had only gotten a seventy on mine, which my parents were not going to be happy about. Plus she reminded us about the essay and I still had no idea what to write, so that was eating at me too. But bigger than that were the problems at the shelter. I knew my mom was right, that there wasn't anything a couple of seventh graders could do, but I still couldn't stop worrying about it. I was lost in thought until I heard a shout.

"Careful!" a man called out. I looked up and saw that a big brown and black dog was racing toward me. I jumped back quickly.

"She's harmless, don't worry," the man running after the dog called. He was about half a block behind.

Knowing the dog wasn't going to bite me, I took a step toward her. "Stop," I told her. "Stop."

The huge dog looked at me, unsure if I meant business.

"Stop," I said in my firmest voice, putting up a hand

to show that I most definitely meant business.

The dog slowed from a run to a walk, her tail wagging.

"Sit," I told her. She came to a stop at my feet and sat, panting.

"Okay, that was amazing," the dog's owner said as he caught up to us, breathing heavily. "I've been telling her to stop ever since she made a break for it at the dog park."

The dog park was four blocks away. "You've had quite a run, haven't you," I said to the dog, holding out my hand so she could sniff me.

"Her name is Coco," the man said, clipping a leash on the dog's collar. "And she's given both of us a pretty good workout."

"Hi, Coco," I said, patting her head. She wagged her tail so hard her whole body wagged with it and then she jumped up to give me a lick.

"Sorry," her owner said, pulling her away and rubbing her back to calm her. "She's still a puppy and she definitely acts like it."

"I don't mind," I said. "I love dogs."

The man smiled at me. "And clearly they love you," he said. "You have a real way with them."

"Thanks," I said. I watched as they walked back down the sidewalk, the dog rushing ahead and her owner trying to keep up. He needed to learn more about leash management but it was clear how much he loved her and that mattered more than anything. Kind of like the Cronins and sweet Humphrey.

I was thinking about Humphrey and dogs like him, with families away at work and school all day, as I started toward the Rox. Then my mind drifted back to the shelter and that's when it hit me. I loved dogs and I was good with them—and that was the solution to everything. Maybe there *was* something a couple of seventh graders could do after all!

9

I was nearly skipping as I walked into the Rox, the smell of coffee, fresh apple pie, and the famous Rox sweet potato fries wafting around me as I headed in. The after-school crowd was already getting started and I waved to Stephan and Gillian, the two servers working.

"Hey, Kim," Stephan said as he swept by, plates of food in both hands. "What's got you smiling?"

"I have a plan," I said happily.

"There's nothing like a good plan," he said cheerfully as he went on to his table.

I headed back to the kitchen, where my mom was working with Alana, the line cook, and my dad was shredding lettuce for dinner salads. The big dishwasher hummed behind them and Colin, one of the guys who worked in the back, gave me a salute as he pulled a steaming tray of dishes out of the machine. Everyone at the Rox was like family.

"Hi, sweetie," my mom said, leaning over to kiss me. She had a light dusting of flour across her cheeks and her curly hair was held back with the polka-dotted chef's hat I got her when I was five. "How was your day?"

"Um, mixed," I said, remembering the pop quiz. I'd tell them about that later. "But I had this really great idea."

"Let's hear it," my mom said, giving me her full attention.

My dad nodded, listening as well. So I started with the shelter needing more money and the Cronins needing someone to walk Humphrey in the afternoon, since my dad didn't know about that. And then I explained the big idea I'd had after running into Coco. As I went on I saw my mom's eyes widen and my dad slowly start nodding his head.

"Honey, that is a fantastic idea," my mom said. "A smart solution to two pretty serious problems."

"It sounds like the perfect fix," my dad agreed. "A real humdinger of an idea."

"Yesterday I said it was too big a problem for kids," my mom said, shaking her head with a smile. "But I think you proved me wrong."

"Way to take charge, Kim," my dad added proudly.

I ducked my head, suddenly feeling self-conscious. But their praise wrapped around me, snug and warm.

Now I just had to find a way to make my plan work.

That night I texted both Sasha and Taylor—I knew I couldn't do this without them. And the next morning in homeroom, I told them my plan.

"We're going to start a doggy after-school program," I whispered excitedly as we stood at the back of the room before the final bell. I couldn't worry about Mrs. Benson's "no talking in the classroom" policy at a time like this. "Families like the Cronins, whose dogs need exercise when they're at work, can sign up to have us pick up their dogs after school. We'll walk them over to the shelter, where they can run around and play with the other dogs until their owners come pick them up at the end of the day."

Sasha's eyes were sparkling and Taylor was beaming.

"The dog owners can pay for the service and that way Alice has enough to keep running the shelter," I said. "And everybody wins."

"They really do," Sasha bubbled, then sent a panicked glance to the front of the classroom. Luckily Mrs. Benson was so busy writing vocab words on the whiteboard that she didn't notice.

"It's totally brilliant, Kim," Taylor added. "You're a genius."

Now I was the one beaming.

Sasha was grinning at the two of us, clearly over-joyed we were finally friends. "Oh, and I just thought of something else," she said. "When the owners come to pick up their own dogs, they'll meet the shelter dogs and maybe want to adopt them."

I hadn't even thought of that! "That would be great," I said.

The bell rang and we started toward our seats, still whispering.

"This dog day care is going to be huge," Sasha predicted. "Seriously the best idea ever."

"You did it, Kim," Taylor said. "You figured out how to save the shelter!"

Now Mrs. Benson was glaring at us. "Girls, if you'd like extra homework, just keep on talking," she said. Extra homework was always her punishment of choice and it worked. I closed my mouth and tiptoed to my desk, quiet as a mouse.

But then Taylor exclaimed. "Kim, you totally just

figured out what to write your paper on!"

And even an extra page of vocabulary from Mrs. Benson couldn't ruin that.

When we got to the shelter that afternoon Oscar made a beeline for Taylor. It was funny to see the sleek gray cat winding his way between all the jumping dogs, but Oscar was a cat on a mission. He passed me and Sasha and put his fat paws up on Taylor's leg, meowing sweetly.

"Hey, there," Taylor said, her Southern accent extra musical as she scooped Oscar up and cuddled him against her shoulder. Clearly she was still more comfortable with cats than dogs.

Even over the noise of Boxer and Lily scuffling for a chewed-up tennis ball and Mr. Smashmouth yipping a happy greeting, I could hear Oscar's rumbling purr. It was as though he was telling Taylor to forget the dogs and focus on him!

After Sasha and I greeted the dogs, with Taylor

giving Lily a good head rub and even petting Boxer, Sasha turned to me.

"Let's tell everyone your plan," she said.

I looked around. Caley and Tim were playing fetch with Hattie while Alice was brushing Popsicle, who wriggled with delight in her arms.

"Maybe we should wait," I said, biting my lip. The thought of explaining it to all three of them at once had me tongue-tied. Plus what if they thought it was a terrible idea?

"Kim, it's an amazing idea," Sasha said, reading my mind like she always did.

"Seriously," Taylor agreed. "They're going to be blown away."

With a cheerleading section like that, who could say no? So the three of us walked over to the others.

"We know about the shelter needing more funding," Sasha began. "And Kim has an incredible idea of what we can do to get the money you need to stay open."

119

My insides were fluttering but just then Lily nudged at my hand, as though she knew that was exactly what I needed. I dug my fingers into her thick fur and the fluttering was gone. I took a deep breath and told Alice, Tim, and Caley everything, starting with my conversation with Mrs. Cronin and ending with the dog after-school idea.

By the time I was done, Tim and Caley were grinning widely but Alice was rubbing her chin thoughtfully, her eyes serious. "I'm not sure," she said slowly. "It *is* a good idea, Kim. But I can think of a number of obstacles."

My heart sank with her words.

"Like what?" Taylor asked. "Because I bet we can solve them." She gave me a quick wink as she spoke.

I grinned back. Having Taylor in my corner was pretty great.

"Well, do you think dog owners will be comfortable letting their dogs run loose with the shelter dogs?" Alice asked.

The wheels in my brain were already spinning. "We

can just do what you do whenever a new dog comes," I said. "Have a trial period and help them socialize and feel comfortable with the group."

"And the owners can meet the shelter dogs," Sasha added. "Seeing what sweeties these guys are will totally win them over." She gave Mr. Smashmouth an extra pat. "And maybe even lead to more adoptions."

"That would be great," Alice said, sounding just the tiniest bit excited at the thought.

Sasha and I shared a smile. One issue down.

"How will you girls coordinate picking up the different dogs and walking them to the shelter?" Alice went on, tucking a stray lock of hair back into her ponytail.

"We can have a weekly schedule, like my mom makes for chores," Sasha said. "We'll write down all the jobs, then decide who gets each dog and brings them here."

"We could even put the schedule up online, like a calendar app," Taylor said. "That way we could all check it from home and you could check it here."

Alice was nodding. "That could work," she said. "But what about getting all the vet records for all the dogs?"

I cast a desperate look at Sasha. It seemed like every solution we came up with was met by another concern from Alice. I was starting to think we'd never convince her.

But then Caley spoke up. "Alice, this idea is fantastic," she said confidently. "It will save the shelter and help these dogs who are stuck home alone all day. Honestly I wish I'd thought of it myself!"

"Me too," Tim added, shooting me a smile. "It's brilliant."

My cheeks heated up and I ducked my head, totally glowing from their praise.

Alice opened her mouth but Caley held up a hand. "We'll figure it out," she said, turning to us with a smile. "I can brainstorm with you guys about the best way to get those vet records."

"I'll help set up the schedule online," Tim said

immediately. "I did one for my summer basketball league and it worked great."

I held my breath as we all turned to Alice, to see what she would say.

Slowly a wide smile broke out across her face. "Kim, I think you might have just saved our shelter."

Sasha and Taylor threw their arms around me while Tim and Caley cheered.

Then Alice, still smiling, broke in. "But it's going to take all of us working hard to make this happen. Especially the three of you, since you'll be in charge."

Sasha, Taylor, and I grinned at each other.

Sasha rubbed her hands together. "Let's start brainstorming ideas," she said. "Like how we'll set things up and how we'll get the word out so people can sign up their dogs."

"Definitely flyers," Taylor said, already thinking ahead.

"Right," I said. Honestly I hadn't even thought about how we'd let people know what we were doing.

The fact that Sasha and Taylor had thought of it proved that Alice was right: it was going to take all of us to make the after-school dog club a success.

"I'm in on the brainstorm," Tim said. "We have to plan out how everything will work before we start soliciting clients." Just then Boxer jumped up on Tim and stuck his tennis ball in Tim's face. Tim began laughing. "Okay, so maybe we can't have a meeting right now," he said, taking the ball from Boxer and tossing it across the room.

"Kim, when should we meet?" Caley said. "We should get this going as soon as possible." Her cheeks were pink with excitement. I kind of couldn't get over the fact that they were so enthusiastic about my idea. I mean, they were in high school but they were acting like I was the cool one.

"Um, how about tomorrow afternoon, right after school, at the Rox?" I said. That was a homework day for me but I was pretty sure my parents would let me start late just this once. They understood how important this was.

"Sure," Caley said. "I can be late to drama for this."

"Works for me too," Tim said as Boxer ran back over to him.

"Sounds good," Sasha said, and Taylor nodded.

"Okay, that's settled," Tim said. "And now I think we should take this crew outside."

Tim, Caley, and Sasha headed for the back door, most of the dogs trailing after them. I was about to follow but then I realized Taylor was standing there, smiling at me.

"What's up?" I asked her.

She replied by throwing her arms around me and hugging me tight. "You are so smart and awesome for coming up with this plan," she said as she let me go. "And I'm so happy I get to be part of it!"

"I'm really glad you're part of it too," I said, grinning at her. Because I was one hundred percent happy she was there. Sasha had been right about Taylor all along. It had just taken me a while to get it.

We started for the back door but then I stopped in my tracks. "You guys, we need a name."

"For what?" Sasha asked.

"For the after-school dog club," I said. "We can't call it that because dogs don't go to school."

Everybody laughed.

"How about Doggy Day Care?" Caley asked.

Tim shook his head. "It's not all day," he said. "Just afternoons."

"What about the Dog Sitter Service?" Sasha asked.

Caley wrinkled her nose.

"You guys, it's obvious," Taylor said, grinning straight at me. "Everything in this town is named Roxbury Park something. So this will be the Roxbury Park Dog Club."

I burst out laughing.

"Perfect," Alice declared.

And it was.

10

When the three of us walked into the Rox the next afternoon Caley and Tim were already there. They'd nabbed a corner booth and had two steaming baskets of sweet potato fries waiting for us.

"Hi, guys," Caley said as the three of us slid in next to them.

"Help yourself to fries," Tim said, his mouth full. "The Rox has the best sweet potato fries in the world."

"Have you actually tasted all the sweet potato fries in the world?" Caley teased.

"I don't have to," Tim said. "It's obvious these are the best."

"Kim's parents own this place," Sasha informed them proudly. "And that sweet potato fry recipe is theirs."

Caley's eyes opened wide in admiration and Tim almost choked on his fries. "I'm moving into your house," he declared when he could talk again.

We all laughed.

"Seriously, what makes these so good?" Caley asked, reaching for more.

"It's a mix of cinnamon and cumin," I said. "And one or two more secret ingredients I can't reveal."

"Later we'll have to kidnap you so your parents will sell us the recipe," Tim said.

"One mission at a time," Caley said, rolling her eyes. "Right now we're saving the shelter with Kim's awesome idea. And we should get started. We have a lot to plan before we can get this club off the ground."

"First things first," Tim said, also ready to get down to business. "How do potential clients contact us?"

"We could put our phone numbers on the flyer," Sasha said, reaching for some fries.

I felt my stomach tighten. "Actually I don't think my parents would be okay with that," I said, worried I sounded like a total baby. "They're pretty strict about who I give my cell phone number to."

Sasha's shoulders slumped. "I didn't think of that," she said. "My mom wouldn't be happy to see my number all over town either."

"Mine either," Caley said, surprising me. "And actually I asked Alice this yesterday. She thinks we should set up a special email account just for the Dog Club and then people who want to call can just use the number of the shelter."

"That sounds great," I said, relieved. "And we can help Alice answer the phone so she isn't the one having to deal with the scheduling and stuff."

"Good idea," Caley said with an approving nod.

I couldn't help feeling pleased at her casual praise.

"What about getting the dogs to the club?" Tim asked, his fingers scraping the bottom of the fry basket. "And also we need more of these."

Caley flagged down Wendy, who ruffled my hair before she scooped up our fry baskets for refills.

"You really are royalty," Tim said, making me giggle.

"Some owners might be able to take a break from work to drop their dogs off at the shelter," Taylor said.

"And maybe those who can't can leave us a key and pay an extra fee to have us pick up their dogs and walk them to the shelter," Sasha added.

Tim was nodding. "I like how you think," he said. "Because the more money we get for the shelter, the better."

I saw Sasha's cheeks turn rosy at his words.

"Speaking of money," Caley said, "I talked to Alice about this too and she said it makes the most sense for her to handle the money stuff—making invoices, collecting payments, and all that."

"Great," Taylor said. "I think that might have been a lot for us to handle."

"Agreed," Caley said.

The fries arrived at the table and we all dug in. They were crisp and steaming and totally delicious. We ate silently for a minute and then Caley looked at her watch.

"I need to get to drama," she said. "Is there anything else we should go over?"

I cleared my throat. "Not to get ahead of ourselves," I said, "but I was thinking we probably need to have a limit of how many dogs we can take."

"Good point," Taylor said.

"Yeah, things could get pretty crazy with twenty dogs running around," Sasha agreed.

Caley and Tim were nodding.

"Kim, what do you think is a good limit?" Caley asked me.

I was pleased to be asked but then thought carefully about her question. "Probably no more than six at a time, at least to start," I said.

"Sounds good," Tim said as he and Caley stood up.

"The fries are on us," Caley said, getting her wallet out. "You guys finish up and we'll see you tomorrow."

"Actually they're on me," I said with a grin.

Caley smacked her forehead theatrically. "Of course, you own the place," she said.

"Which is why we'll be hanging out with you all the time," Tim said with a wink.

After they'd gone Sasha grinned at us. "This is really happening, you guys," she said.

Taylor raised her glass of ice water. "To the Roxbury Park Dog Club," she said.

Sasha and I raised ours as well. "To the club," we cheered.

"This is for you," I said to Mrs. Cronin on Monday morning as I handed her one of the flyers Sasha and Tim had made.

She took it just as her phone rang.

"You can read it later," I said as I snapped Humphrey's leash on.

"I will," she promised as she clicked on her phone.

Humphrey and I made our way down the driveway. The sun was shining but it was cooler than yesterday. Fall was definitely coming.

"Today you get three of us," I told Humphrey, who barked joyfully when he saw Sasha and Taylor walking up to us, their arms piled high with more flyers.

They both knelt down to greet Humphrey, who rolled over for a good belly scratch.

"I put these up all around my neighborhood last night," Taylor said. "And my dad put some up at Old Farm Market when he went shopping last night."

"Great," I said. Old Farm Market was on the edge of town and most people in Roxbury Park did their big grocery shopping there. A lot of people would see that flyer.

"My mom said she'd put some up in the break room at her office," Sasha said, giving Humphrey one last rub before I tugged on his leash to get him walking. "And in some of the other stores near town that are too far for us to walk to."

"She's not worried about you being around even more dogs?" Taylor asked with a grin.

Sasha rolled her eyes. "Of course she is," she said. "I had to promise I'd never, ever forget my shelter clothes and that I'd shower twice as long after."

Taylor and I laughed.

"My mom is so embarrassing," Sasha said with a sigh.

I reached over with my free hand and patted Sasha's shoulder. Most of the time she just laughed about her mom's rules but I knew there were times when it got to her.

"At least she doesn't call you Sugar Plum in public like my dad," Taylor said.

I tried not to laugh but then I caught Sasha's eye and we both burst into giggles.

Taylor grinned wryly. "It sounds funny but it's the

most mortifying thing ever when he does it at school."

"You *are* sugary sweet," Sasha said, and Taylor pretended to punch her in the arm. That got Humphrey excited and he began to bark.

"Settle down, girls," I said in my best Mrs. Benson imitation. It wasn't very good but they laughed anyway.

It was really fun to be in on the joke with Taylor and Sasha.

We turned onto Main Street and Sasha and Taylor began to hang flyers.

"So will your parents put up flyers at the Rox?" Sasha asked, securing one to the bulletin board at the park entrance.

"They said they'd do it first thing this morning," I said. My parents had been really excited when I showed them the flyer and the email we'd written, and promised to do all they could to help.

"Excellent," Sasha crowed. "Everyone in town goes to the Rox."

We continued down Main Street with Sasha and

Taylor papering every telephone pole and bulletin board with a flyer.

"So that's done," Sasha said, after the last flyer had been hung and we were on our way back to the Cronins'.

"What else can we do to get the word out?" Taylor asked.

"I was thinking we should put up flyers at all the vet offices in town," I said, almost tripping over Humphrey, who had stopped short to sniff a candy wrapper. I pulled him forward before he could try to lick it.

"Good idea," Sasha said. "And we should do the pet stores too, for dog owners getting food and stuff."

"Definitely," I agreed. "Like the Pet Emporium."

"Oh, good idea," Sasha said.

"Can you guys think of anywhere else?" I asked.

They both shook their heads.

"I think after this we wait," Sasha said. "And get ready to start taking calls."

We were almost back to the Cronins' and Humphrey was moving a bit more slowly.

"Do you want breakfast, Humphrey?" I asked.

His sweet brown eyes opened wide and he began trotting, his nails clicking on the sidewalk.

Sasha and Taylor burst out laughing.

"I've never seen him move so fast," Sasha said.

"All it takes is the right motivation," I said, chuckling as Humphrey raced up the porch steps as fast as his short legs would take him.

Mrs. Cronin was still on the phone when she came to the door so I didn't get to ask her about the flyer. I was pretty sure she'd look at it though. And the way we'd papered Roxbury Park with flyers, I felt confident that a lot of people would read about our Dog Club.

The question was, would any of them actually sign up?

That afternoon when we got to the shelter Alice called us to her office for a meeting. We filed into the cozy space, which had a cluttered desk on one wall and a small, lumpy sofa set across from it. The walls had pictures of all the dogs who had been at the shelter. One of my favorites was of Sammy, the dog my family adopted when I was little. And I noticed a new one of Mr. Smashmouth and Lily cuddled together under a tree that was really cute too.

Today Alice had on a white T-shirt covered with rainbow dog paw prints, and there were dark circles under her eyes, as though she'd been up late the night before. "I made a new section on our website," she said. "It took me a while since this computer is so slow but I think it turned out well." She turned the computer screen so we could see it. Roxbury Park Dog Club was at the top and then there was a section explaining the club and the service we offered.

A jolt of electricity zipped through me as I read it. It looked so professional!

"Awesome," Taylor said with a grin.

"I think it covers everything," Alice said. "And I put in an email address just for the club, and the number of the shelter so dog owners can get in touch, for questions and for scheduling. You guys can be in charge of that."

"Perfect," Sasha said happily.

"We're all pitching in," Alice went on. "And I'm always here if you need me. But the club is yours and it's going to be hard work to run it."

I felt a sliver of worry at her words but Taylor was nodding. "We're ready," she said.

Alice smiled. "I know you are and I know you can handle it. And I *am* here to help, so never hesitate to ask."

We all nodded. I appreciated Alice saying that and I knew we'd need her help sometimes. But I really liked the club being ours and I wanted to handle everything we could by ourselves. I wanted to show Alice and everyone else that we could do it.

"Let's go over everything you'll need to be on top of," Alice said.

"Wait, let me just get my notebook so I can write this down," I said, realizing that if we were going to be in charge, we couldn't forget anything.

Alice waited, an approving smile on her face, until I'd gotten a notebook and pen out of my backpack, and then she went on. "First there's what you'll need to find out from prospective clients, before we let them sign up for the club."

I nodded, writing down every word.

"We need to make it very clear that we have to have vaccination records from every dog," Alice said. "All dogs who come must be vaccinated and spayed or neutered, no exceptions. We also need to let them know that every dog at the shelter is spayed or neutered and up to date on their vaccines, so clients don't have to be concerned about that."

"Sounds good," Sasha said.

"We'll tell people the club starts next Monday," Alice said. "To give us a week to iron out any last-minute details."

"Great," I said. It was so exciting to think that by this time next week the club would be up and running!

"Then there's making sure you have contact information for all the owners, in case you need to get in touch with them," Alice went on.

"Maybe we can make up a list that attaches to the schedule," Taylor said. "That way we all have it on our phones when we're out walking the dogs and on the office computer here."

"Good idea," Alice said. "You girls are going to do a great job. The next step is getting calls and clients, and then we'll take it from there."

"Great," I said, closing my notebook and putting it away.

Alice stood up. "Now go ahead and have fun with the dogs."

The three of us headed out and were warmly greeted by Lily, Boxer, and Hattie. I noticed Taylor knead Boxer's head affectionately and I grinned. She had come a long way!

"Let's take them outside," Sasha said.

So we headed into the yard with the dogs, now

joined by Mr. Smashmouth and Popsicle, bounding ahead of us. I threw a tennis ball and all five dogs raced after it.

Sasha picked up the Frisbee so there would be something else to chase, but then made a face. "I think this toy might be over," she said.

I looked over and saw that it was nearly split in half. "Yeah, the sharp edges could cut the dogs," I said.

Sasha walked over to the garbage under the porch to get rid of the useless toy. "Won't it be great when we have enough money to buy some new balls and stuff for the dogs?" she asked.

"As long as the club actually works," I said.

Taylor squeezed my arm. "It will," she said.

I really hoped she was right.

Sasha found Boxer's favorite green Frisbee, which was in better shape, and began throwing it for Boxer and Lily, while Hattie and Popsicle were having a friendly tussle over a rubber bone. I was happy to see Hattie being a little more independent. And watching her made me think of something else. Caley, Tim, and Alice had helped us with setting up the club, like how to run it and all the details we needed to tell clients so that the dogs would be safely cared for. But there was a whole other set of details, things that we'd need to be on top of if we wanted the club to work. "I think we should have a club notebook," I said.

"But we're doing the schedule online and contact information online," Sasha said. "Couldn't we just put any notes up there too?"

"We could, but Alice's computer is really slow and I'm not sure she'll want us using it all the time," I said. "And, if it's a notebook we can pass it around between all of us and take turns writing in it at night and stuff."

"Plus we can make it pretty," Taylor said with a grin. "An online document can't have stickers and drawings and stuff."

Sasha laughed. "Okay, you guys are right," she said. "We clearly need a dog notebook, not something online.

What exactly are we going to be taking notes on?"

"I was thinking it could be stuff about each dog," I said, "like anything special they need while they're here. Like if Hattie were a client we could write about how she needs to work on being independent from Lily."

"Or what kind of games they really like," Sasha said, catching on immediately. She was so into the idea she didn't notice Boxer had brought back the Frisbee till he nudged her with his nose. She laughed and gave it another toss. "That's a great idea, Kim."

"It is," Taylor agreed. "Each dog can have a page and I can take pictures of them and we can glue them in." She looked slightly uneasy as Boxer bounded up but then she stepped forward and took the Frisbee to throw for him. Boxer wiggled his hindquarters in expectation, then took off after it the second it left Taylor's fingers.

"Perfect," I said, thinking back to my dog collage. "Maybe we can even do a little research on their breeds, so we know more what to expect from them and what they need."

Sasha was about to add something but then we heard Alice calling us from the porch steps.

"Good news," she called happily. "The Roxbury Park Dog Club just got its very first client!"

11

Alice was smiling as we raced over and ran up the porch steps. "And Kim, they said you know their dog very well."

"Oh, the Cronins," I guessed breathlessly.

"Yes, a basset hound named Humphrey," Alice said.

"I'm so glad Humphrey will come!" Sasha said. "He'll love it here."

"He really will," I agreed. I was already thinking

about his entry in our club notebook, all the things that helped get him to be active and get the exercise he needed. All the things besides being told "breakfast"!

Hattie came running over to us, the Frisbee in her mouth. I was about to take it from her to begin another game of fetch, but then I heard the office phone ringing again. I remembered we were supposed to help out with club calls. "Want me to get that?" I asked Alice.

"Sure," she said. "If it's a shelter call just put them on hold, but if it's a call for the club, go ahead and take down the information on the pad that's out on my desk."

I ran into Alice's office, Sasha and Taylor right behind me, and grabbed the phone off her desk.

"Is this the Roxbury Park Dog Club?" a woman asked after I'd said hello.

"Yes," I practically shrieked. Then I realized how unprofessional that sounded and I cleared my throat. "Yes, this is Kim of the Roxbury Park Dog Club," I said in my most serious voice. "How can I help you today?"

Sasha gave me a thumbs-up as she and Taylor headed back to play with the dogs.

"I'm Ellen Whitman and I'd like to sign my poodle Clarabelle up for the club," she said. "She gets lonely when my husband and I are at work and I think she'd enjoy the time with other dogs."

"Yes, I'm sure Clarabelle will love it here," I said. I took a deep breath and then ran through all the things Alice had talked about, like the vet records we'd need plus more about how the club worked. "And for an extra fee we can pick up Clarabelle and walk her here."

"That would be great," Mrs. Whitman said. "That way I wouldn't have to leave work. You'd just need to be sure to take your shoes off when you go inside to get her leash."

"Okay," I said. We had to take off shoes at Sasha's house too, so that dirt from outside didn't spread. I wondered how Mrs. Whitman cleaned Clarabelle's feet after a walk. She probably had a special rag or something.

"I'll need your address so we can plan a pickup time."

I saw Alice had written in the Cronins' address in the notebook on her desk, as well as the time they'd drop off Humphrey's vet records on the top of the page. I made sure to get the same information from Mrs. Whitman.

"I'm looking forward to meeting Clarabelle," I said. "All of us here love dogs and we'll take great care of her."

"I'm counting on it," Mrs. Whitman said.

The second the call was officially over I squealed and Sasha and Taylor ran over. "We have another client!" I exclaimed. "A poodle named Clarabelle."

"The Whitmans live just down the street from us," Sasha exclaimed. "Clarabelle is really sweet."

And then the phone rang again. "Oh, let me get it this time," Sasha begged, and Taylor and I waved her over.

"Roxbury Park Dog Shelter," Sasha said in a businesslike tone that would make her mom proud. She paused while the person on the other end of the call spoke and then she grinned. "Yes, you've reached the Roxbury Park Dog Club and I'd be happy to tell you about it."

Taylor and I high-fived as Sasha began to tell the next potential client about our club.

It was official: The Roxbury Park Dog Club was taking off!

"Kim, this is not your best work," my dad said, the corners of his mouth turning down as he looked at my quiz, the one where I gotten a seventy. I'd put off telling my parents but I knew it would come out at Parent Night in a few weeks, so I'd finally bitten the bullet and confessed. It was later that night and we'd just finished washing the dinner dishes. Matt was out with a friend.

My mom had her arms crossed over her chest but she didn't look angry, just disappointed, as she leaned against the counter. "Kim, I'm worried that all the time with the Dog Club is taking away from your home-work," she said.

My dad was nodding as he put away the salad bowl. "We know you want to help out at the shelter and we think the club is a great idea," he said. "But school has to come first."

My heart thumped hard in my chest. I couldn't let them take away my time with the club, not now, when we were really starting to make it happen.

"It's not, I promise," I said. "I'm just having a hard time because Mrs. Benson says the quiz questions so fast. But I'll get the hang of it, I know I will."

My parents exchanged a look and I rushed on. "Mrs. Benson says the quizzes aren't a big part of our final grade. The tests and the essay count for more. And I did well on the first test because she gave us enough time for it. And I really studied."

"That's good," my dad said, sounding slightly less worried.

My mom raised an eyebrow. "How is the essay going?"

I gulped because I couldn't lie to my parents. "I think I've figured out what I'm going to write about, mostly, and Matt said he'd help. I'll work really hard and I know I'll do a good job." Okay, that last part was kind of a lie since I didn't *know* I'd do a good job. But I really would try my hardest.

They were communicating with their eyes again and I held my breath. Finally my mom nodded. "If you promise to work harder on those quizzes and do well on the essay, you can keep on working at the Dog Club."

I let out a cheer.

My dad held up a finger. "But if your grades start to slip because of the time you're spending with dogs—"

"They won't," I interrupted. "I promise."

My mom smiled. "And we believe you."

I headed upstairs before they could change their minds. I'd already done my homework but I was going to look over our reading one more time. I knew we'd have a pop quiz the next day and this time I'd be ready for it!

Over the next few days we got calls from a bunch of dog owners interested in finding out about the club. Some decided the club wasn't for them and others took down information and then said they'd be in touch. By the time Monday rolled around we had five dogs attending the very first session of the club. Over the weekend their owners brought them by the shelter so they could socialize with the other dogs, and the owners could see where their dogs would be going. Each dog had done well so we were set to bring them all in to start the week. And most of the owners had requested pickup service, which meant even more money for the shelter. It also meant we had to go get them right when the bell rang at the end of school.

We split up as soon as we got out of the building and headed to get the dogs, each of us going to a different part of town. I went by Humphrey's house first. I heard his nails clicking on the floor as soon as I opened the door and when he saw me he gave a loud bark of joy.

"I'm happy to see you too," I told him. He licked my face as I snapped on his leash. "Ready to go make some friends?"

He bobbed his head as we headed out. I almost forgot to lock the Cronins' door but luckily remembered when we were halfway down the front path. It would not have been good if they got home to find their front door open!

"First we're going to pick up Gus," I told Humphrey. "He's just a few houses down. Maybe you've met him out walking or in the dog park."

The Cronins had told Gus's owner, Mrs. Washington, about the club and she had signed him up right away. He was a brown Lab who bounded about happily when Humphrey and I arrived at the front door. His leash was right on the front hall table and he stood still, trembling slightly with excitement, as I clipped it on his red collar. As soon as we started for the door he barked in delight. It made me so happy to see his excitement at going out in the afternoon, when he was usually just home alone.

Things got a little tricky once we hit the sidewalk. Gus wanted to run but Humphrey preferred his own, slow pace. It took several firm tugs on Gus's leash for him to understand that I meant business.

As we walked down Main Street I heard a dog barking loudly and a moment later I saw Sasha nearly being dragged down the street by Coco, the big black and brown dog I'd almost been run over by the week before. I'd been really pleased when her owner called but now it looked like she might be more than Sasha could handle.

I wanted to rush over and help but Humphrey and Gus had stopped to sniff the doorway of Rose Petal Bakery and weren't interested in budging.

"Tell them like you mean it," I called to Sasha as two nervous-looking people crossed the street to avoid Coco.

"I've tried that so much I think I'm losing my voice!" Sasha called. Her hair was slipping out of her braid and her face was red. "And my arm is about to fall off from trying to keep a strong grip on her leash."

I gave Humphrey's and Gus's leashes a tug and managed to get them moving. "Coco, sit," I said in my most take-charge dog voice as I got close.

Coco looked up, a playful glint in her eye.

"Sit," I said again.

Coco sat.

"I don't know how you do that," Sasha said, rubbing her arm and then leaning over to rub Coco's head so she'd know she'd done a good job.

"Kim knows how to show dogs who's boss," Taylor said, coming up behind us. We'd just had her pick up one dog, Clarabelle, a classically groomed poodle with clouds of fluffy white fur on her paws, upper body, and head, while the rest of her was cleanly shaven.

"I thought I did too, but Coco didn't seem to get the message," Sasha said as we started for the shelter.

I was about to respond when Humphrey stopped short and Clarabelle almost tripped over his leash. Coco began barking at a squirrel across the street and Gus tried to sniff Clarabelle, who backed away uncertainly.

Sasha began to laugh. "And I thought walking the dogs to the shelter was going to be the easy part!"

Taylor and I began laughing too as we got our pack moving and in the front door of the shelter.

Lily, Boxer, Hattie, and Mr. Smashmouth were in the middle of greeting Daisy, a dachshund with short brown fur, but they took one look at their guests and began barking while Popsicle ran yipping into Alice's office.

I turned to Sasha. "I think maybe the walk *was* the easy part," I said as Alice hurried out of her office.

But Sasha couldn't hear me over the din. Caley came over and led Hattie and Clarabelle off to one corner while Tim headed outside with Boxer, Coco, and Lily. Taylor soothed Popsicle and Sasha began a game of fetch with Gus and Daisy. And finally things were calm again.

"I guess we need to work on our entrance," I said to Alice. I was a little worried she'd say the club was too much chaos and we'd have to stop it, but she just smiled.

"It's a lot to have all of them come in at once," she said, absently brushing some fur off her T-shirt, which had a silhouette of a Doberman and said, "Wag Like You Mean It." "Maybe think of ways to stagger it next time."

"Good idea," I said, relieved she was taking it in stride.

I looked around the shelter to see where help might be needed. Taylor and Popsicle were snuggling happily on the far side of the room and Sasha's game of fetch was going well. But over in the corner it looked like Hattie and Clarabelle were not hitting it off. There was a red ball between them and they clearly didn't want to share it. The fur on Hattie's neck was standing up and

Clarabelle stood in a defensive pose. Caley didn't appear to notice the warning signs and was walking away to get another toy.

I bit my lip as I took in the scene. I didn't want to step on Caley's toes, or seem like I was telling her what to do when she was in high school and I was just a kid. But the dogs needed my help and that mattered the most. So I took a deep breath and headed over.

When I got close I saw Hattie's ears flatten and she gave a low growl. "Hattie, no," I said in my most forceful dog voice. I wrapped my fingers around her collar so she couldn't snap at Clarabelle. She was worked up and breathing hard, but stayed still.

Caley had heard the sound and rushed over to hold on to Clarabelle.

"Whoa, I so didn't see that coming," Caley said, her eyes wide.

I was rubbing Hattie in long soothing strokes and her breathing began slowing to normal. "The way Clarabelle had her ears back in that defensive stance was a sign she was upset," I said. "But it can be hard to notice."

"What was going on?" she asked.

"A struggle for dominance, I think," I said. "It's pretty common when dogs first meet each other. And for Hattie it's a threat to have a new dog in her home."

"I guess that makes sense," Caley said. "But what can we do about it?"

"They'll determine who the alpha dog is," I said. "The dog in charge. But we need to let them know who the pack leader is. That's what I did when I came over and stopped them."

"You really are the dog whisperer," Caley said admiringly.

Normally I loved hearing that but right now I was trying to read the signs between the two dogs, to see if they were ready to try and play together or if they needed some space. Hattie had relaxed but Clarabelle still looked tense.

I reached out my hand to Clarabelle. We hadn't

really met yet so letting her sniff my hand was the best way to introduce myself and say hello. After a moment she reached out and gently touched her nose to my palm. I let go of Hattie and pet Clarabelle softly, feeling her slowly calm down.

"This is Hattie," I said to Clarabelle. "And this is Clarabelle. I think the two of you may have gotten off on the wrong foot, so let's start over. I know you're going to be good friends soon."

"Do you think I can let her go now?" Caley asked.

I looked at both dogs and nodded. This time they just began sniffing each other and after a moment, Hattie rolled over and showed her belly.

I smiled. "They've decided Clarabelle is the alpha here," I said, relieved it had gone so well. "They should be fine now."

Sure enough, after I tossed the red ball they ran after it together happily.

Caley shook her head. "Good thing it wasn't Coco and Boxer who got off on the wrong foot," she said.

Which made me realize I wanted to look outside and see how the biggest dogs were doing. I left Caley with Hattie and Clarabelle and went to look out a back window. Tim was running after Boxer, who had nabbed his favorite green Frisbee, while Coco and Lily jumped around them in a gleeful circle, barking joyfully. The sight of it made me smile.

"Wow, what was going on with Hattie and Clarabelle?" Sasha asked me as she and Taylor came up next to me.

I told them the story.

"Yikes," Sasha said. "It's really lucky you noticed."

"Yeah," I said. "But we can't count on luck if we're running a business."

Taylor was nodding. "It's true," she said. "How can we avoid conflicts like that in the future?"

I'd been thinking about it. "First maybe we need to change how we bring the club dogs to the shelter," I said.

"It was pretty overwhelming today," Sasha agreed.

The red ball rolled close to us and she picked it up and tossed it for Clarabelle, Hattie, and Mr. Smashmouth, who had joined them.

"It might help if we bring the dogs in a few at a time, instead of all at once," I said. "And let them acclimate for a bit before the next dogs arrive."

"That would let the shelter dogs get used to visitors, too," Taylor added.

"Exactly," I said. "I think Hattie felt threatened by all the newcomers at once. From now on she'll feel more comfortable with Clarabelle but it will still be a better transition for all the dogs."

"And when new dogs come," Sasha said.

"Yeah," I agreed, twining a lock of hair around my finger. "And maybe we should spend some time now integrating the other dogs. They met this weekend but let's help them feel safe playing together."

Sasha nodded. "Great idea. I can take Hattie, Lily, and Clarabelle outside," she said.

I shook my head. "Let's keep Hattie away from Lily

a little longer," I said. "She's really been getting more independent and we want to help her. What about taking Gus and Daisy with Taylor while I bring Popsicle over to play with Hattie and Clarabelle?"

So that's what we did and the rest of the afternoon went smoothly.

12

After we left the shelter we took a quick trip into town. Our parents had agreed we could have a half hour to buy our Dog Club notebook and start writing at the Rox before Taylor and Sasha had to go home for dinner (and in Sasha's case, a post-shelter shower).

"Oh, how about this blue one?" Taylor asked, taking an aqua notebook off the shelf at Greenway Stationery.

"I'm not sure there are enough pages in it," I said.

"What about this one?" I pulled out a tan notebook with two hundred pages.

Taylor wrinkled her nose. "It's ugly," she said.

"We can decorate it," I said.

"Yeah, but we'll still be able to see that tan that looks like the walls in Mrs. Benson's room," she said.

I looked at the notebook again and realized she had a point. I put it back on the shelf immediately. "Right, no way we're getting that one."

Sasha laughed. "The last thing I need is to be reminded of school in our precious hours away from it."

Sasha didn't have trouble with school like I did but it wasn't as if any of us liked Mrs. Benson. The good news for me was that I'd done a lot better on our last pop quiz. Now if I could just get the essay done I'd be set. But I'd worry about that later.

"None of the other notebooks are big enough," Taylor said, flipping through them.

"What if we get a binder?" Sasha asked. "That way we can add pages as we need them."

"Oh, good idea," I said. I walked over to the binder section and took a red one off the shelf. "How about this one?" I asked.

Sasha and Taylor nodded.

"And it doesn't remind anyone of school?"

They both laughed and shook their heads.

We grabbed some dog stickers and a pack of paper, then went up to the counter to pay.

"Hey, there, Kim and Sasha," Mr. Pepper, the owner of the store, said. "It looks like your twosome has become the three musketeers."

I grinned. "This is Taylor."

"Pleased to meet you," Mr. Pepper said. "I'll look forward to seeing you around."

"Thanks," Taylor said with a smile.

We paid and I tucked the binder and paper into my backpack.

"Everyone's so nice here," Taylor said when we were back on the sidewalk, headed for the Rox.

"It's true," I said, feeling proud of Roxbury Park. It

really was an awesome place to live. "Maybe that's why we name everything after our town," I added with a grin.

Taylor and Sasha laughed as we walked into the Rox. We settled into a booth and my mom came out of the kitchen to bring us a steaming basket of sweet potato fries.

"Mom, this is Taylor," I said, reaching for some fries.

"It's a pleasure to meet you, ma'am," Taylor said.

I could tell my mom liked Taylor's Southern manners because her eyes were shining as she smiled at her. "It's nice to finally meet you," she said. "I've heard Kim and Sasha raving about the magnificent Taylor."

"And I'm even better than they said, right?" Taylor asked, grinning.

"Her modesty is one of her best qualities," I said.

My mom and Sasha laughed.

"These fries are incredible, Mrs. Feeny," Taylor said, taking one out of the basket.

"I'm glad you like them," my mom said. "One of these days you'll have to come over for a real meal."

Taylor smiled. "I'd like that," she said.

I knew I would too. And I could tell by the huge grin spreading across Sasha's face that she felt the same way.

My mom headed back to the kitchen. I realized we didn't have much time left so I wiped my fingers on a napkin and pulled out our new Dog Club binder. "Let's get started."

We made a page for each of the five dogs, then wrote down some of the things we'd observed over the day.

"Humphrey moves around more when he's playing with Gus," Sasha said.

"Yeah, I noticed that too," I said, writing it down. "We should definitely make sure they spend a lot of time together."

"We don't want to let our Humphrey get lazy," Sasha agreed. "Well, lazier anyway."

"Daisy got pushed to the side a little when Boxer and Coco were playing fetch," I said, still writing. "So we should find ways to include her more."

"Maybe make sure she plays with some other dogs?" Taylor asked.

"Yeah," I agreed. "And Hattie was a little more independent today. I saw her following Humphrey around."

"That's a cute set of doggy friends," Sasha said, grinning.

"I think Humphrey liked her too," I said.

Sasha's cell phone rang. "It's my mom," she said. "I have to go."

She slid out of the booth while clicking on the phone, waving to us as she left.

"I should get going too," Taylor said. "My dad is cooking up his famous fried chicken."

"Sounds good," I said.

"We'll have to have you over for dinner the next time he makes it," Taylor said. "You haven't lived till you've eaten real Southern fried chicken."

"I'd love that," I said. It would be really fun to meet Taylor's family. And introduce her to the rest of mine.

I waved as she headed out. Then I bent down over our notebook, adding every detail I'd noticed during the very first club meeting at the shelter. We'd hit a few rough patches, which made sense for the first day. But I wanted everything from here on out to be perfect.

It rained Wednesday morning but by the time we got to the shelter, club dogs in hand, the sun was shining. As planned Sasha arrived at the shelter first, while Taylor and I took the long way around with our dogs. Tim and Caley came next, with Coco. The three of them settled their dogs in and were ready to help when I showed up with Humphrey and Gus. Taylor came last with Daisy, who moseyed over to Lily and began a happy game of tug-of-war with a brand-new plastic bone.

"I got some new toys," Alice said as she came out of her office. She was wearing her "Peace, Love, and

Dogs" shirt, which was becoming my favorite. "Much needed, I have to say. And I got rid of the ones that were truly falling apart."

"Great," I said, looking around and seeing several new balls, chew toys, and pull toys.

"I held on to Boxer's green Frisbee though," she said, smiling. "He'd be heartbroken if I got rid of it."

We all agreed with that.

"It's so nice out after all that rain," Sasha said as Alice went to take Popsicle for a walk. "Let's all go outside."

"Great idea," Taylor said. "Running around sounds good after that quiz in English."

Sasha stuck out her tongue. "Two pop quizzes in a row is not fair," she said.

"Tell me about it," I agreed. This quiz had caught me by surprise and I had missed two of the answers. Which wasn't that bad but I'd really have to stay on top of my reading if I wanted to keep my quiz grades up. Plus there was the essay to worry about. It was due a week from Monday and I still hadn't figured out how to get started writing it.

We told Tim and Caley our plan for the afternoon. They stayed back to work on some office records for Alice while Sasha, Taylor, the dogs, and I headed outside. I picked up a new tennis ball from the bin on the porch and threw it, laughing as most of the dogs took off after it. Soon we were all racing around in the big yard with the pack of dogs. Boxer and Coco stuck together in their pursuit of the green Frisbee while the others raced after tennis balls that Taylor and I kept throwing as soon as one dog brought one back. Now that Alice had replenished supplies we had a lot of them.

"Ugh," Taylor said as Lily enthusiastically rubbed a muddy ball on her clean jeans.

"Looks like someone else needs shelter clothes," I said, laughing.

I grabbed the ball and tossed it into the far corner of the yard, where it landed with a wet smack in a mud puddle left over from the rain earlier. Lily had gotten lured into a tug-of-war game with Gus, but Hattie and Clarabelle, who were now fast friends, raced for the muddy ball. A moment later they were back, covered with mud and wriggling with joy.

"What is going on?"

A sharp voice cut across the yard and all of us, dogs and humans alike, froze. A tall woman in spiky heels and a perfectly tailored white dress was standing on the porch, her face twisted as though she had just smelled a dead rat.

I was closest to her so I cleared my throat. "The dogs are playing," I said, hoping it didn't sound too obvious. I wasn't really sure what she meant since it was clear what was going on.

"But why is my Clarabelle, who was just groomed yesterday, completely filthy?" she asked.

Yikes. This must be Mrs. Whitman. Her eyes narrowed as she took in the scene. I followed her gaze and saw that Clarabelle's snowy cloud-puffs of fur had turned into soggy, muddy messes. And I realized that for Mrs.

Whitman, with her classically groomed dog and rules about shoes in the house, this was a very bad thing. I just wished I'd realized it earlier, before we took Clarabelle outside. Now it was too late.

"Hello, Mrs. Whitman," Sasha called weakly.

"Sasha, I'm surprised your mother would allow you to work in a place like this," Mrs. Whitman said. "Where is Alice? Isn't she the one in charge here?"

This was going from bad to worse.

"I'm Kim," I said, hurrying up the porch step. I reached out my hand but then realized it was covered with mud and snatched it back quickly. "Sasha, Taylor, and I run the club." I realized I had a streak of mud on my face that was drying in a crusty line. I probably looked completely irresponsible to glamorous Mrs. Whitman.

Sure enough she took a step back to keep her distance. "There has to be more than just a group of children in charge," she said disdainfully. "And you should know better than to let the dogs run about willy-nilly. I'd like to speak to Alice immediately."

I gulped and ran inside for Alice. Luckily she had just gotten back and was hanging up Popsicle's leash. "We have a problem with one of the customers," I told Alice, feeling awful. I had wanted to show her we could handle the club and instead I was begging for her help on only the second day.

But Alice just nodded, smoothed her hair, and followed me to the back porch.

"Aren't you the person who is supposed to be overseeing this operation?" Mrs. Whitman snapped.

Clarabelle was still chasing Hattie and had leaves clinging to her fur and a tuft of grass stuck to the top of her head. It would have been funny if it didn't mean we were in even worse trouble.

"What seems to be the problem?" Alice asked in a calm, firm voice, the one that dogs instantly obeyed.

Sure enough Mrs. Whitman's tone was more polite as she explained that Clarabelle had just been groomed.

"Perhaps in the future you could communicate

with us about such things," Alice said. "But I think it's also important that you understand dogs at the club play inside and out. We will never let them get injured or participate in anything unsafe, but they may come home a bit messy."

"Well, then I'm not sure this is the right place for us," Mrs. Whitman sniffed.

"Perhaps not," Alice said diplomatically. "And I'm sorry if the parameters of the club weren't clearer when you joined. Kim, can you help Mrs. Whitman get Clarabelle ready to leave?"

Alice didn't sound upset but my cheeks were flaming as I called Clarabelle over, then brought her in and snapped on her leash. Mrs. Whitman snatched it out of my hands and left without a word, careful not to let her dog's fur touch her outfit. I had sick feeling in my stomach as the door shut behind her.

What if all the other customers hated what we were doing and took their dogs away too?

13

Things were more subdued for the rest of the afternoon, at least as subdued as they can be with a bunch of energetic dogs running around. I tried to lose myself in the fun but I couldn't stop worrying about what was going to happen when the other owners showed up for their dogs. At this point every dog was pretty muddy.

Mrs. Cronin was first. Alice brought her out to the porch and my throat tightened as I watched her seek out Humphrey, who was playing fetch with Popsicle and Gus. When she saw him, her face lit up.

"He looks so happy," Mrs. Cronin said, coming up to me and putting an arm around my shoulders. She didn't seem to care about how muddy I was or that Humphrey's paws looked like they had been dipped in chocolate. "I love to see him like this."

I relaxed against her, feeling like I could breathe for the first time since Mrs. Whitman had come.

"Yeah, I think he's really enjoying himself," I said.

Sasha came up, her face dotted with sweat. "Want to throw the ball for him?" she asked Mrs. Cronin.

Mrs. Cronin was still dressed for work in her heels and suit but she took the ball without hesitating and tossed it for Humphrey and his new friends. They all took off after it, Humphrey chugging along on his short legs.

Mrs. Cronin burst out laughing at the sight. "Thank you for this," she said. "I hated thinking of him stuck home alone and now I know he'll be here, having fun with his doggy friends and getting the exercise he needs. It's perfect."

Just then Mrs. Torres came into the yard and Daisy ran up to her, barking. Mrs. Torres rubbed her knuckles along Daisy's head while greeting her lovingly. When she was done she looked up at Sasha and me with a grin. "I can tell someone had a good time at Dog Club," she said.

"Yeah, I had trouble keeping up with her," Taylor said, coming up to us. I noticed a small twig stuck on one of her braids and I pulled it out for her.

I was finally feeling better, now that two owners were so happy with the club. But the thought of what had happened with Clarabelle still needled at me.

"So what did these guys get up to?" Mrs. Cronin asked as Humphrey headed back to Popsicle and Gus.

As Sasha began to fill her in on the day, a new idea came to me, an idea that just might prevent any more situations like the one with Clarabelle.

14

As soon as the final owner had come for Dog Club pickup, Alice called us into her office. We filed in and sat on the sofa but I stayed perched on the edge, eager to spill my new idea.

"There's something I think we should do," I blurted out before Alice had even sat down in her desk chair. "So that we don't have any more unhappy owners like Mrs. Whitman." As soon as the words were out I realized that since Alice had called the meeting she probably wanted to be the one to start it. But she smiled and nodded at me to continue, so I did.

"Actually, first I want to say I'm really sorry about what happened with Clarabelle, Alice," I said. I still felt bad whenever I thought about Mrs. Whitman snapping at Alice.

But Alice shook her head. "No need to apologize," she said. "Sometimes dogs get dirty when they play. We do need to make some changes about how we communicate with the owners, so there aren't surprises like that. And that's what I wanted to talk to you guys about. But Kim, it seems like you've already thought of something, so let's hear it."

I took a deep breath and jumped in. "Okay, so you know how when Mrs. Torres and Mrs. Cronin got here they asked all about what their dogs did at the club?" I was bouncing a little on my seat as I spoke. "I was thinking we could have a section on the website where we post messages about all the stuff the dogs do every day."

"I love that!" Sasha exclaimed. "Like we could

write about how Hattie and Daisy love playing with the new green ball and spent forty minutes playing fetch together."

"Exactly," I said, grinning. Sasha always got exactly what I was thinking.

"We could take pictures and post them too," Taylor added. "So the owners could really see what goes on here at the club."

I grinned at her. She was pretty good at getting my ideas too.

"We could post every day, so the owners would always have an update on what their dogs did each day," I said. "And any potential clients who want to know more about the club will see it too. That way there aren't any surprises about what goes on at Dog Club."

"If an owner who wants her dog to stay neat reads about a day of fetch in the yard after a rainstorm, and sees a picture of Humphrey looking like he rolled in a pigpen, they know exactly what they're signing up for," Taylor said with a grin.

I nodded, laughing.

"And the owners whose dogs attend the club can get a good sense of what their dogs have been up to," Alice added, her eyes shining. "It's a terrific idea, Kim. And I'd be happy to show you how to post it on the shelter's website."

I finally sank back against the sofa, relief coursing through me. Yes, we'd had a setback, but we'd figured out how to move forward!

A few minutes later we said good-bye to Alice, Tim, and Caley, and headed outside. The sun was low in the sky, casting a golden glow over Main Street. We waved to a group of kids from school as they passed us. They had clearly come from a baseball game in the park, and were walking with their gloves and bats slung over their shoulders.

"I love the idea of writing up what the dogs do every day," Taylor said, pulling her pink hoodie closer around her shoulders as a cool breeze blew by. "And I was thinking we should give it a name."

"How about the Roxbury Park Dog Update?" I joked and they both laughed.

"I think we need to leave Roxbury Park out of this one," Taylor said with a grin.

"What about Notes from the Dogs?" Sasha asked.

Taylor frowned. "That sounds like we're teaching the dogs to write notes to people."

I laughed. "I think she's right," I told Sasha, who pretended to sulk.

"I was thinking we could call it the Dog Club Diary," Taylor said.

I nodded and so did Sasha, though a bit reluctantly. "It *is* better than mine," she sighed theatrically.

Taylor grinned. "You could try to teach the dogs to write if you want," she said.

They both laughed but something else was occurring to me. "You know, Alice was right," I said slowly. "The club is a lot of work."

Sasha frowned. "Yes, but it's worth it," she said quickly.

"Definitely," I agreed. "I'm just thinking maybe we should divide up the work we do, so we're not all trying to do everything."

Taylor nodded. "That makes sense," she said. "Also if just one of us is in charge of something, it will definitely get done."

"And that way we don't each have too much to do," I said.

"We all have to walk the club dogs to the shelter and take care of them there," Taylor said. "So that we can't divide up."

"What are the other jobs?" Sasha asked.

"Well, now there's the Dog Club Diary," I said. "Posting to it every day and also setting it up and running it—basically being a web designer."

"That's a lot of work," Sasha said. "I think it should be a two-person job."

I nodded. "I think you're right. There's also answering calls and emails from potential clients and scheduling them. And keeping the client list updated."

Taylor and Sasha were nodding. Then Sasha spoke up. "Kim, I nominate you to write for the website. You have all those great observations about what the dogs like and what they need. And you tell good dog stories. I think the owners will really like reading what you write."

"Agree," Taylor said immediately. "That's totally your job, Kim."

"Thanks," I said, pleased at their praise. "I'd love to do that. I think it'll be really fun."

"And I can do the web design stuff," Taylor said. "I like computers. And you know I like taking pictures."

"Perfect," Sasha said. "So that leaves the calls, client list, and scheduling to me. And I'm on it."

"Great," I said, grinning.

We started walking down Main Street.

"You know, I think we just had a business meeting," Taylor said.

"It did feel awfully professional," Sasha agreed. She slung an arm over each of our shoulders.

"Maybe we should branch out and form a cat club next," Taylor joked.

"Let's do something easier, like fish," Sasha said, making us all laugh. The cool air felt good on my face as I walked down Main Street with my two best friends.

"One thing's for sure," I said.

"What's that?" Sasha asked.

"Us," I said. "We really are the three musketeers."

Sasha grinned. "I think so too."

"Me three," Taylor said, and we all laughed.

At the next Dog Club meeting we decided that the club dogs were ready to arrive at the shelter at the same time. The three of us plus our charges met up in front of the shelter. There was happy barking when we walked in but it wasn't crazy like it had been before. As soon as Humphrey's leash was off, he padded over to Popsicle, Gus right behind him. Coco and Boxer had a joyful reunion that involved a lot of jumping around while the other dogs began an elaborate greeting of sniffing.

I was about to start playing with them when I noticed something unusual. Alice, Tim, and Caley were all standing in front of the office smiling. And they were all wearing sweaters, or in Tim's case, a gray sweatshirt.

"Alice has a surprise," Tim said. He looked at Alice and Caley. "Ready?"

They nodded and then all took off their sweaters at the same time. When I realized what was going on, I gave a shriek of delight. Sasha clapped her hands together and Taylor gave a low whistle. "Pretty neat," she said.

The three of them were wearing different-colored T-shirts that said "The Roxbury Park Dog Club" in big letters, with matching paw prints.

"I designed them," Tim said. "What do you think?"

"I love them," I bubbled, and Sasha and Taylor quickly agreed. I couldn't believe two high schoolers were wearing shirts to advertise the club that I'd thought of. It was so cool!

"I picked the colors," Caley said, like she wanted some credit too.

"They're perfect," I said, and she smiled like my praise really mattered to her. It was the best feeling.

"This is totally my favorite of all your dog shirts," I told Alice.

"I'm glad to hear it," she said. "Because there's one for each of you too." She held out three folded shirts.

"Thanks," Sasha squealed, taking them. Taylor and I echoed her thanks as we ran to the bathroom to change into our new shirts. When we unfolded them, we saw there were dogs on the back, too.

"I like this version of shelter clothes," Sasha said, preening in the bathroom mirror after she'd put hers on.

"Yeah, me too," I agreed, looking at my reflection. "I think the dog on the back looks like Humphrey."

"Because he's so lazy," Taylor laughed.

"I think it's awesome that two high school kids are wearing shirts for our club," I said, still feeling the glow from Tim's and Caley's enthusiasm.

"Seriously," Sasha said, looking as happy about it as I felt.

"Why wouldn't they?" Taylor asked, still not as impressed with the older kids as Sasha and me. "It's the coolest club around."

"Good point," I said with a grin.

"It really is a cute shirt," Sasha said, smoothing it down as she gazed at her reflection in the mirror.

"Maybe the Dog Club should have a fashion line," Taylor kidded.

The three of us headed out to the main room and began an afternoon of blissful dog play.

15

Way less blissful was the essay. The pressure was really on, not just to get it done but for it to be perfect. If I got a bad grade I knew my parents would ask me to spend more time doing homework, which would mean less Dog Club time. Plus this was my first big assignment for Mrs. Benson and I had to show her I could do it. But the more I thought about it, the more I realized that I didn't just need to do a good job for Mrs. Benson and my parents. I needed to prove to myself that I could handle the big seventh grade essay. So all of that together? A whole lot of pressure!

I wanted to put it off as long as possible but I knew that would be a big mistake, so Friday night after dinner I went up to my room to write. My desk was covered with books, information I'd printed out for the Dog Club notebook, and papers. I cleared everything off, turned on my computer, and stared at the screen, which was as blank as my mind. I mean, I knew I wanted to write about the Dog Club, but should I just jump in with that? Or start somewhere else? Then there was the question of which things were important and which weren't. Mrs. Benson had made a big deal about "not going off on tangents and sticking to the heart of things." But how did you know the difference?

After five minutes of my mind running in circles I decided to get my writing juices flowing by working on the first entry in the Dog Club Diary. That turned out to be way easier than the essay. I wrote about how Coco, Popsicle, and Gus had made a game of snatching

Boxer's green Frisbee. Taylor had taken a picture of all four dogs running gleefully around the yard and I knew we'd post that. But I tried to describe it too, how funny it was to see such different-sized dogs frolicking together. Then I wrote about Daisy playing ball with Hattie and Taylor. I didn't write about how Taylor tripped over a branch and ended up with leaves stuck to her braids, but it had been pretty funny. Sasha and I helped pull them out and made a lot of jokes about our grooming service. Last I wrote about how toward the end of the day the dogs had flopped in a big pile together with the three of us, just snuggling and getting love. Writing about it let me remember how fun it all was and I realized I was going to love working on the Dog Club Diary.

I saved it and then emailed it to Taylor so she could upload it to the site, along with pictures. And then I went back to the essay. I stared at the screen, pushing myself to think of something, anything, to say. Why was this so hard but the Dog Club Diary entry so easy?

I jumped as I heard a knock on my door. I turned

in my desk chair, feeling annoyed that one of my parents was already up to check on me. But to my surprise it was Matt who walked in, wearing his favorite old Star Wars shirt and smelling like the apple pie my mom had heated up for dessert, which Matt had eaten almost half of.

"What's up, Pip-squeak?" he asked, picking up one of the china dogs from my collection.

"Don't call me that," I snapped. "And don't touch that."

"Okay, calm down," he said, setting down the dog and raising up his palms.

"Sorry," I said. "I'm just stressed about this essay."

"How's it going?" he asked, flopping down on my bed. Clearly all was forgiven. Matt wasn't one to hold grudges and I knew he understood how hard I worked at school stuff.

"Awful," I whined. "I don't know how to start or what parts I should write about or anything."

"But you have a ton of things to say," he said.

"It doesn't feel that way," I said.

He laced his fingers behind his head and looked up at the ceiling. "You're thinking too hard."

"How can you think too hard?" I asked, puzzled.

"When you worry so much about how something should be that you can't actually start it," he said.

"Oh," I said, getting it. "Yeah, I guess that's me."

"You just need to write what you do at the shelter," he said. "Start by telling me first. Sometimes it's easier to talk about it and then begin writing."

"I can do better than talk," I said, swiveling in my chair and pulling up my Dog Club Diary entry on my screen. "I can show you."

Matt hauled himself off my bed and read my post over my shoulder. "This is great," he said. "Exactly what you need for your essay, though that should probably be a little more structured."

"I can't just write about playing with the dogs," I said. "That doesn't answer the question of how I make a difference at my volunteer work."

"Two things, little sister," Matt said. "First, yes it does, because those dogs would be really lonely without you playing with them. That *is* you making a difference."

"I never thought about that," I said. "But I guess it makes sense."

"Second thing," he said. "Tell me more about the setup. Because that scene is about more than just you playing with dogs."

"What do you mean, the setup?" I asked.

"How you ended up at the shelter with a mix of dogs with homes and shelter dogs," he said. "Because the shelter wasn't set up like that when you first got there."

"You mean the Dog Club," I said. "How me and Sasha and Taylor started the Dog Club."

Matt shook his head. "No, how you saw a problem facing the place you were working," he said. "How you came up with an idea to save it and then did the work to make that idea happen. And how well it's been going ever since."

"Oh—" I started again, but Matt quickly cut me off.

"And how you worked together with other people," he said. "Because essays like this should always include something about teamwork."

I leaned back in my chair, considering all he had said. Then I smiled. "Matt, you're a genius," I said.

"I know," he said. He gave me the peace sign as he headed out.

Finally, I started to write. And once I started, I realized that just like Matt had said, I had a ton of things to say.

I began with the most important thing: the dogs. How great the shelter was and how fun it was to play with the dogs. I included what Matt had said about how important it is for dogs to be played with and loved. Then I wrote about Humphrey and dogs like him who faced long hours alone.

I took a quick break and grabbed some oatmeal cookies in the kitchen. It turned out that writing made you really hungry. But as soon as I was done, I headed back upstairs to my computer. I wrote about the shelter potentially having to close and how I'd come up with the idea for the Dog Club. Writing it made me remember how scared I was to tell Alice about it but that I'd worked up my courage and done it. And she had listened and let us give it a try.

Next I wrote about all the work Sasha, Taylor, and I had done to get the club started. Which got me thinking about Taylor and how just a few weeks ago she'd seemed like a threat and now she was one of my best friends. And that too was because of our work at the shelter. That's when I realized that my work at the shelter wasn't just about dogs. So when it came time for my conclusion, I wrote about that too.

When I first volunteered to work at the Roxbury Park Dog Shelter, I thought I would get to have fun with dogs and learn more about caring for them. And I definitely have. But I've learned a lot more than that too. I've learned about how to be a friend. I've learned how to step up and try to make a difference when someone, a dog or a person, needs help. I wanted to try to help the dogs at the shelter and I'm happy that my friends and I were able to do that with the Roxbury Park Dog Club. But the shelter helped me too. It helped me learn to trust my own ideas, to speak up when I think I have something to say. And it taught me that both dogs and people are worth getting to know, even when it doesn't seem like it at first. So I'd have to say that while I think I have made a difference at my work, my work has made a difference to me too. And one thing I know for sure: I can't wait to see what happens next!

I worked on my essay all night and on Saturday morning I revised it. I was pretty proud of how it had turned out. I was just doing a final spell-check when I heard another knock at my door. This time I was hoping it was my parents and sure enough, they both walked in, looking slightly anxious.

"We wanted to see how the essay is going," my mom said.

"And to see if we can help at all," my dad added.

"Actually, I think I'm done," I said. "Want to read it?"

"Yes," they said practically in unison.

I printed it out and then waited nervously while they sat on the bed and read it together. My mom smiled at a few parts and once my dad laughed. That was probably the part about how funny it was to see such different dogs play together. Then at the end I heard my mom sniff a little. And that's when I knew my essay was okay.

"Kim, I'm so proud of you," my mom said when she was done. She had tears in her eyes.

"You had a great idea," my dad said. "And you worked your tail off to make it happen."

Normally I rolled my eyes when my dad came up with one of his corny sayings but today it didn't feel quite so corny. Because I had really worked my tail off to start the Roxbury Park Dog Club.

"So I can keep spending time working on the club?" I asked.

My mom nodded. "If you keep doing top-notch work like this, absolutely."

"I will," I promised.

"It really is amazing how you came up with the idea that saved the shelter," my mom said, pulling me down on the bed between them so they could both hug me.

"And then you wrote a bang-up essay about it," my dad added, kissing me on top of my head.

I had to roll my eyes at that. But I hugged them back too. Having my parents this proud of me felt really good.

Monday afternoon the shelter was filled with yelps of happiness and playful dogs. As soon as we let him off his leash Humphrey padded over to Popsicle, while Coco made a beeline for Boxer. Hattie, who had been so much more independent lately, was chasing after a ball with Daisy. And Lily and Mr. Smashmouth had come over to snuggle with the three of us, which we were very happy about.

"I love this," Taylor said, her arms around Lily.

"Yeah, I don't think it gets any better than all this dog time," Sasha agreed. She had Mr. Smashmouth on her lap and was rubbing his fluffy belly.

I looked around at all the dogs. "It's pretty amazing," I said.

Sasha and Taylor both looked around too. And then we beamed at each other. "We made this happen," Sasha said proudly.

"Photo moment!" Taylor called, pulling her phone out of her pocket. We leaned together, the dogs snuggled between us, and Taylor snapped.

"This will be perfect for your photo wall, Kim," she said in a satisfied tone as we all looked at the shot. Our faces were close together and we were all laughing, looking like the happiest three musketeers around. Which we pretty much were.

"It is," I agreed. "And I want it as my screen saver on my phone."

"Oh, me too," Sasha exclaimed.

Taylor grinned and bent over her phone, her braids falling down with a musical tinkle of beads. "I'm sending it to you guys right now."

Just then the phone in the office rang. "I'll get it," I said, scrambling up. "Hopefully it's another client."

I ran into Alice's office and picked up the phone. "This is the Roxbury Park Dog Shelter and Dog Club," I said in my most professional voice. "How can I help you today?"

A few minutes later I hung up, just as Alice was walking in. "We have a new customer," I told her happily.

Alice grinned. "That's great news," she said. "And guess where I was?" She went on before I could answer. "The hardware store. I made an appointment to get the floors redone. We've been needing to do that for ages, and thanks to you and the club, we can afford to take care of it."

"Awesome," I said, grinning widely.

"Good news?" Sasha asked as I sat back down with Sasha, Taylor, and the dogs. Hattie came over and put her head in my lap.

"We have a new client," I said. "Sierra, a German shepherd mix." I went on scratching behind Hattie's soft ears. "Her owner read the Dog Club Diary and said it sounds like the perfect place for her dog since she and her husband work long hours. She's really excited."

"Awesome," Sasha said. "The more customers we get, the better for keeping the shelter open."

"And better for the dogs too," I said. "So they can keep making new friends." Hattie had rolled onto her back so I could pet her belly and she was panting happily. "You'd like that, wouldn't you, girl?" Hattie reached up and gave me a lick on my hand.

Taylor laughed. "I used to think it was a little strange

how you talked to dogs," she said. "But now I see that you don't just understand them—they understand you too."

"Kim the dog whisperer," Sasha said affectionately.

"I think we all do some dog whispering around here," I said.

"Kim, my dad's heard all about you and he says it's high time he met my other best friend," Taylor said. "He insisted I invite both of you over for a sleepover Friday night."

"Sounds great!" Sasha enthused.

"Totally," I said. I liked being called Taylor's other best friend. And I was really looking forward to meeting Taylor's family. "Will there be Southern fried chicken? I heard it's the best around."

"Yes," Taylor laughed. "Plus greens and biscuits. Anna even said she'd make her famous strawberry shortcake."

"I can't wait," I said, my stomach rumbling at the thought of all that good food.

"I just hope we have room for milk shakes," Sasha said.

"Milk shakes?" Taylor asked, her brow crinkled.

"That's our sleepover tradition," I said, happy at the thought of sharing it with Taylor. Who knew what fun add-ins she might come up with. There could be all kinds of great Southern sweets I didn't even know about.

"We start with the ice cream and milk," Sasha said. "And then we add all kinds of stuff, like Reese's Pieces and Cap'n Crunch."

Taylor smacked her lips. "I'm in," she said. "And I can't believe you think we wouldn't have room for that."

"Seriously, Sash," I mock-scolded. "Like there's ever been a time you couldn't finish a milk shake."

Sasha laughed.

Boxer pranced over, Coco right behind him, and dropped a tennis ball at my feet. I stood up and tossed it and the pile of dogs around us suddenly all leaped up and streaked after it. Soon we were all running around, throwing balls and playing with the dogs.

Later, when the owners started arriving for Dog Club pickup, I noticed Mrs. Cronin playing tug-of-war with Popsicle. I was surprised to see that Mr. Cronin was there too, rubbing Humphrey's belly and watching his wife play with Popsicle. I walked over to them.

"She's a sweetie, isn't she?" I asked, reaching down to pet Popsicle. In the short time she'd been at the shelter she'd already gotten bigger, with a plump puppy belly. "Humphrey adores her."

"Yes, we read about that in the Dog Club Diary," Mrs. Cronin said, grinning at her husband, who smiled back. "So we wanted to come down and meet her for ourselves. And now that we have, we've fallen in love. Which means that you are going to have two dogs to walk in the morning. We're adopting Popsicle!"

I knew it wasn't professional but I couldn't help myself: I threw my arms around Mrs. Cronin.

Sasha and Taylor came running up. "Popsicle has a new home," I told them joyfully. "The Cronins are adopting her!"

Sasha and Taylor threw their arms around the two of us as Humphrey and Popsicle and then some of the others came over to join the celebration.

Because that's what it was: a celebration of the shelter, of the club, and of an abandoned puppy finding a new home.

But most of all it was a celebration of all that was yet to come, all the good times ahead at the Roxbury Park Dog Club.

KEEP READING FOR A SNEAK PEEK AT

THE NEXT DOG CLUB ADVENTURE!

Sasha has always wanted a dog, but her mom isn't convinced she's responsible enough to take care of one. Can the Dog Club help Sasha prove she's ready for a pet of her own?

1

"I just heard about the greatest pet," I said to my mom. We were sitting in the breakfast nook of our sunny kitchen eating English muffins; it was the perfect time to reveal my latest plan to convince my mom we needed a pet.

Mom was taking a long sip of coffee but she looked at me over the rim of her mug and raised her eyebrows, waiting for me to go on.

I took a deep breath. "A de-scented skunk," I announced.

My mom made a sputtering noise as she tried to keep from choking on her coffee.

I hid my grin by taking a bite of English muffin. This was exactly the reaction I was hoping for.

"A skunk?" Mom asked, her voice shrill. "People actually welcome skunks into their homes?" She glanced around at our immaculate kitchen, where everything was in its place and every surface was free of dust and crumbs. My mom was all about our house being clean, which was why she had shot down every request I'd ever made for a pet.

But I was determined that this time would be different.

"Yeah," I said. "They're very affectionate."

My mom shuddered at the thought of cuddling with a skunk.

"And they're clean," I adding, laying it on thick.

She shook her head. "There is no way we are getting a skunk."

"Okay," I mumbled in my most disappointed voice, slumping down in my seat but casting a quick glance

3

at my mom. Just as I'd hoped she looked concerned. Yeah, my mom had a ton of rules about cleaning and homework and screen time, but I knew how much she wanted me to be happy. Ever since she and my dad had split up when I was a baby it was just the two of us and I knew how hard she worked to get me things like American Girl dolls, and send me to summer camp and dance classes. But the thing I wanted more than anything was a pet, which was why I'd come up with this whole plan in the first place. It was never about a skunk, it was about a—

"Well, then what about a hamster?" I asked, like the thought had just occurred to me. "Hamsters live in a cage and look cute."

"Their cages need wood shavings," my mother said, frowning slightly at the thought of the dust wood shavings might create.

"Actually now they have paper shavings that hardly make a mess at all," I replied. I'd done my research.

"What about the odor?" my mom asked, wrinkling

her nose as though she could already smell a dirty hamster cage.

"We could keep the cage in my room," I said. "And I'd clean it every day so it would stay fresh."

My mom stood up and began to clear her place. "Hurry up with that English muffin, honey," she said. "You don't want to be late."

I was so eager to do what she asked that I stuffed the rest of my food in my mouth. Then I saw her wince. Whoops. Yes, I'd finished the muffin, but I'd forgotten to use good table manners, one of the many things that mattered to my mom. Honestly sometimes it was hard to get everything just how my mom wanted it. It didn't help that she was perfect, from her neat clothes and our spotless house to her job as a successful lawyer. I got my less-than-perfect genes from my dad, who lived in Seattle. When I visited him during school vacations there were dishes piled in the sink, comfortable clutter on every surface, and we always chewed with our mouths open. Not that I'd want to live with my dad; I was happy here in Roxbury Park. But it might be nice if just once in a while my mom relaxed enough to leave a few crumbs on the counter or something.

"Really, Mom, you wouldn't even know the hamster was there," I said as I rinsed off my dishes in the sink and piled them neatly in the dishwasher, trying to make up for the muffin thing.

"A pet is a lot of work," my mom said, filling a travel mug with coffee for her drive to work. She added a half teaspoon of sugar and then secured the lid.

"I know, but I would do it all," I said. "I'd use my allowance to buy hamster food, I'd change the water every day, I'd clean the cage, everything."

My mom glanced at the clock on the stove. "We'd better hurry or we'll be late," she said.

For a moment I wondered if I should let it go and wait until later to push for the hamster. I didn't want to make us late. But I'd come this far and the skunk decoy really seemed to have worked. I needed to see it through now, before my mom could come up with other reasons not to get the hamster.

"Okay," I said, following my mom down the hall to the foyer. I'd left my pink backpack in its designated spot on the bench by the door, next to the rack where we kept all our shoes. Inside the house we did socks and slippers only. "But Mom, what about the hamster? I really think I'm ready for a pet. I'm old enough to take care of it all on my own and I promise you won't have to do a thing."

I held my breath as I waited for her to answer.

"Honey, no," she said, the one word puncturing all my hopes.

"But why?"

"Sash, I know how much you want a pet," Mom said. "But I don't think you're ready. A pet is a huge responsibility: it's a living creature and it depends on you completely."

"I can handle it, I know I can," I said quickly. I was positive I could, if only she would give me a chance.

But my mom was shaking her head.